Leatherby Manor

Judith Ellis

First published 2022
by Rowanvale Books Ltd
The Gate
Keppoch Street
Roath
Cardiff
CF24 3JW
www.rowanvalebooks.com

A CIP catalogue record for this book is available from the British Library.
Paperback ISBN: 978-1-913662-97-4
E-Book ISBN: 978-1-913662-98-1

Thank you to Mark, who was called upon regularly due to my lack of IT skills. The problem on most occasions was a Picnic Error. This apparently was, I quote, a "problem in chair not in computer".

Also to my bestie Roberta, who was happy to provide feedback at the end of every chapter.

Love you both x

Table of Contents

Chapter 1

Martha waved goodbye to her mother and younger sister for the last time. The minute she turned the corner, they would be out of sight. She was on her own now, and at sixteen years old, she was about to be employed as a housemaid at Leatherby Manor.

It was a bright September morning as she made her way to begin the next chapter of her young life. She worked hard to suppress her apprehension, but she was unable to control the nervous excitement she felt in her stomach. It was quite a walk to the manor house, but the weather was unseasonably warm for September, and it was heavenly to be strolling through the countryside in glorious sunshine. She stopped at the top of the small village situated below the imposing manor and took a sharp intake of breath at the sheer size of the building. It reigned over the tiny village with complete dominance. How on earth would she find her way around a house of that size?

She continued walking along the cobbles. Flowers adorned the quaint thatched cottages that lined either side of the street, and there was a bustling atmosphere amongst the small local shops. A steep incline surrounded by gardens led to the manor house. There was an impressive display of meticulously maintained flower beds and a thriving variety of trees, shrubs and bushes. The path was edged with sweet-smelling escallonia iveyi, dramatic in its appearance with lush, green, glossy leaves and delicate clusters of white blooms.

"Morning, lass. You must be the new housemaid."

The voice startled her as the man pushing a wheelbarrow seemed to have appeared from nowhere.

"I'm Albie, head gardener on this fine estate," he said, with pride in his voice.

"Hello, nice to meet you. I'm Martha." She smiled and politely offered him her hand.

He nodded his head and shook her hand enthusiastically. "I'll walk with you, lass, to the servant's entrance. Mrs Harvey will be waiting for you."

His wheelbarrow had the most persistent squeak, which Martha found a little annoying, but she was happy to be in his company. Together, they entered the small courtyard at the side of the main house, which led to the servant's entrance.

"Just knock," Albie said and then continued in the direction of the potting shed.

Martha climbed the three steps leading to the door, straightening her hat and smoothing down her dress. She looked a lot younger than her sixteen years. She was petite in stature with vibrant, wavy auburn hair held in a ponytail by a shiny, emerald-green ribbon. Her hazel eyes complemented her hair, and her rosy cheeks gave her a youthful glow.

Before she had a chance to knock, the door opened. Standing in the doorway was a tall, slender woman wearing a long-sleeved black dress edged with a white collar. Around her waist was a thick black belt, which held a large bunch of keys. The few strands of dark brown in her hair had become overshadowed by grey. It was neatly drawn back and pinned at the nape of her neck.

"You must be Martha. Welcome to Leatherby Manor. My name is Mrs Harvey; I'm the housekeeper." She moved aside, allowing Martha to enter. "Follow me to the servant's hall—I'm sure we can arrange a drink and something to eat."

Martha liked her straight away.

There was a lot of loud chatter in the servant's hall, which immediately stopped when they both entered.

"Everybody, this is our new housemaid, Martha," Mrs Harvey announced.

Martha glanced around, feeling a little self-conscious. All eyes were on her.

"Hello," she said, very quietly.

She was introduced to the first footman, Arthur; Rosie, one of the other housemaids; and the kitchen maid, Elsie. At that point, a very short, rotund woman appeared, her unruly grey hair trying desperately to escape from underneath her cap. From her full-length apron, Martha assumed she must be the cook.

"Come with me, lass. I'm Mrs Mead, the cook—I'll find you something to eat," she said, ushering her to the kitchen.

She placed some ham, cheese and bread on the table in front of Martha, along with a cup of tea.

"Tuck in, lass. You've come a long way, got to keep your strength up."

By the time Martha had finished her food, Rosie appeared.

"Follow me," she said, looking towards the staircase leading to the servants' quarters, which were situated on the top floor of the manor.

Rosie was tall and slim with raven hair carefully plaited then coiled and held with a large clip. Her blue eyes and long black lashes were captivating to the point of being hypnotic. Coupled with her milky white complexion, she was striking.

She explained that the male servants used the same stairs, but their sleeping quarters were kept separate from the female quarters by a locked door. The only two people with keys were Mrs Harvey, the housekeeper, and the head butler, Mr Hampton, who Martha had yet to meet.

"I'll leave you to settle in," Rosie said, and she turned and walked out of the room.

Martha stood in the centre of the tiny attic room and looked around. There was a single bed, a wardrobe, a bedside cabinet and a chest of drawers, on top of which sat a large jug of water, a bowl and a towel. The bed had a wrought iron headrest and was neatly made with clean white linen and a thin, washed-out grey blanket tightly tucked into the mattress.

She walked across to the window, which looked out onto the servants' courtyard and across sprawling green fields. Rosie was outside, laughing in the company of a footman, but it wasn't the one Martha had been introduced to earlier, whose name she had already forgotten.

Suddenly, a sturdy-looking gentleman dressed in a long black jacket, white shirt and black tie approached them. At his arrival, the footman acknowledged him and then made his way quickly back indoors. Rosie followed, and the courtyard became quiet.

Martha unpacked the few items she had brought from home, hung her coat up and left the room to join the other servants. When she arrived at the bottom of the stairs, she was about to enter the servants' hall when a gong sounded, which caused much activity. Two maids rushed past her. Rosie explained that the gong indicated to the family that it was time to dress for dinner. The two young women were Ethel and Muriel; they were lady's maids. They hurried upstairs, one to dress Her Ladyship and the other to dress Lady Emily.

One of the other maids, Nell, returned from the village and introduced herself. She looked older than Rosie but didn't seem quite as confident. She was softly spoken with a friendly disposition, but she was not blessed with Rosie's good looks. Her hair didn't have a definite colour; it was a muddy blonde and had been pulled back into a thin ponytail that looked lifeless and lacked lustre. She was shorter than Rosie and definitely plumper. Her apron was pulled taut across her chest; a larger size would have been more flattering. Martha chatted with her, and it soon became clear that they both enjoyed a happy family life. Nell confessed that she missed her family dreadfully and it had taken her many months to come to terms with being away from home.

Martha had been brought up well; her family were good people, church-going people, who worked hard. She wanted to make them proud and hoped she would have more success at settling into her new life than Nell.

"Right, young lady, I think you need to have a good night's rest after the long day you've had," ordered Mrs Harvey. "The laundry maid has placed your uniform in your room. Tomorrow you will shadow Rosie; she will show you the ropes. Now, run along."

As the evening progressed, Martha became noticeably more tired. It had been a busy day, and she was more than happy to bid goodnight to everybody and was glad to be climbing the stairs to bed.

She slept surprisingly well in her new surroundings and woke feeling refreshed and ready to begin her day. It was 5:30 a.m. Her working day would end at 10 p.m.; the return to her bed seemed a long way off.

"You ready, Martha?" Rosie called. "It's time we were downstairs."

"Yes, all ready," she replied, making her way to the door.

Rosie stared at Martha; her uniform was way too big for her tiny frame.

Martha gestured helplessly at her baggy dress. "I know," she said, and both girls laughed.

"Muriel will soon whip that into shape for you. She takes care of all the alterations for upstairs and downstairs."

They made their way to the housekeeper's room. Nell had already arrived for duty. It was Mrs Harvey's job to check the housemaid's boxes for supplies. Once that was complete, the three girls left to start about their work.

"Drawing room first," Rosie declared.

All three girls climbed the stairs, making their way to the main entrance hall. Rosie opened the door, and Martha stepped out of the servant's quarters.

"Amazing, isn't it?" Rosie said, holding the door open.

Martha had never seen anything so splendid. The walls were adorned with bold paintings and tapestries. Above the sturdy wooden front door, the Leatherby coat of arms took pride of place. The grand, carved mahogany staircase appeared to extend forever.

She crossed the hall, entered the drawing room and was greeted with a large, ornate inglenook fireplace. The windows were dressed in heavy, pale-green velvet drapes, and an elaborate crystal chandelier sparkled in the early morning sunshine in the luxuriously decorated room.

Rosie scowled. "Martha, stop gawping. We have a lot to do."

They set to work. First, the curtains were drawn back and given a forceful shake. Next was the arduous task of cleaning the fireplace. Rosie explained that the ashes must be raked, the hearthstone washed and the coal bucket put into the hall for the footman to collect and refill. The small rugs were to be taken outside and shook; the carpet needed to be hand brushed and the wooden floor swept.

"While the dust settles, which takes about fifteen minutes, we move on to the library, then return to dust the drawing room," Rosie said, while Martha looked on, struggling to make a mental note of all the instructions.

By the time the family arrived downstairs for breakfast, all chores would need to have been completed. Rosie reminded Martha that housemaids were never to be seen in any of the public rooms by the family. And she must not speak to any members of the household unless she was spoken to first.

"How do you remember everything?" Martha asked, sounding anxious.

"You just do," Rosie replied nonchalantly.

Well, that hasn't helped me at all, thought Martha, wishing Rosie had been more helpful.

When the heavy cleaning was complete, the two maids changed out of their drab grey aprons and into pristine white ones.

"Now it's time to call the family," Rosie said as she squeezed past Martha to make her way back upstairs.

"When do we eat breakfast?" Martha asked, following behind Rosie. She was now ravenous.

"Not yet," was the reply, with no indication as to when.

Hot water was taken to each bedroom washstand. It was customary for the married women of the house to take their breakfast in their bedrooms; the single ladies attended breakfast in the dining room. Today, however, Her Ladyship had an early appointment so she had instructed the staff that she would be eating with the rest of the family and a breakfast tray was not required.

"Now, we eat." Rosie smiled as they rushed downstairs, leaving the family to dress for breakfast.

There was lots of commotion in the kitchen, but the servants' hall was quiet. The only servants eating were Martha, Rosie and Nell. They sat around a large trestle table big enough to accommodate all the servants at once. Compared to the elegantly decorated and colourful rooms upstairs, the servants' hall was especially dingy. The one good feature was the welcoming fire. Above the mantelpiece was a photograph of King Edward VII and Queen Alexandra; no other ornaments or pictures decorated the drab cream walls. At the far end of the room, an impressive wooden dresser held neatly organised cutlery and crockery. There were just two comfy armchairs, which were placed either side of the fireplace; the remainder of the seating was wooden hard-back chairs. The window was so high it was impossible to see the courtyard from inside the dreary room, but at least it allowed the sun to shine through.

"Rosie, have you anything to report this morning? And how was our new recruit?" Mrs Harvey asked. Her authoritative stance filled the doorway.

"Nothing unusual to report, Mrs Harvey, and I think Martha will do very nicely," Rosie replied, glancing at Martha and giving her an encouraging smile.

"Well, come along, girls. Almost time to return upstairs. The family are already halfway through their breakfast. There is still work to be done in the bedrooms."

The three girls returned to their duties. The bedroom windows were opened and the bedding thrown back for the beds to air. Hot water bottles were emptied along with any slop in the wash-hand stand and chamber pot. Fresh towels were placed, and a general tidy of the room was made. Then came what Martha decided was the worst job of all: the raking of the ashes. Lastly, the beds were made and the feather pillows plumped.

In addition to the daily cleaning, each main room would need to be "turned out", some on a weekly rota and some fortnightly. This involved moving furniture and brushing curtains. Picture frames were to be cleaned with cotton wool and fine furniture and floors rubbed. The bed linen was changed and gathered into a bundle in preparation for the laundry maid; this would normally take place on a Saturday.

The days were long with a routine of arduous work. Chores were expected to be completed to the highest standard. If they weren't reached, the chore was repeated until the required standard was met. Ten o'clock each night was a welcome release, but all too soon the day would begin again.

Downstairs was always a hive of activity, and Martha soon found herself swept up in it. Days and weeks rushed past her until suddenly a month had gone by and, though at times she missed her family, she had settled well into the vigorous daily routine.

The gentleman in the long black coat whom she had seen in the courtyard on her first day was Mr Hampton, the head butler. He was well respected by all the servants and ran a tight ship, always happy to help but expecting nothing less than your best. His voice was rich with authority, matching his stern appearance. He displayed a sallow complexion and deep-set eyes. His salt-and-pepper hair was precisely cut and oiled into place, his dress was immaculate, and he expected the exact same approach from his footmen.

Arthur, the first footman, reminded Martha of her older brother. He had a quiet nature and kept himself to himself. His duties were performed impeccably, and he never failed to look flawless in his uniform. He was tall and lean with perfectly groomed hair.

Charlie, the second footman, appeared quite flippant towards his duties. He didn't take the same pride in his work as Arthur did and made it perfectly clear (on numerous occasions) that he had no intention of remaining a footman all his life. He was slightly shorter than Arthur with curly blond hair, which at times appeared unruly. "Control that hair, young man," was an instruction that could be heard from Mr Hampton on a regular basis.

Charlie was a good-looking young lad, and he knew it. His cheeky grin and sparkling blue eyes certainly attracted attention. His infectious personality filled the servants' hall; he was fun to have around.

Martha envied Ethel and Muriel, the lady's maids, and wished that one day she too might hold a position of such, in her eyes, high standing. Although she had never met any of the family, it had been easy for her to build a picture in her mind of Her Ladyship and Lady Emily just by the conversations she'd had with Muriel and Ethel.

There was never any mention of Lord and Lady Leatherby's son, William. The only reference made to him was that he didn't live there. Nell had neatly skirted Martha's questions about him, and even Rosie stayed tight-lipped.

Rosie was a good worker and quite sure of herself but could be a little bossy at times, especially to Nell. Although Nell was older and had worked at the manor house longer, she didn't share Rosie's self-assurance. She didn't stand up for herself and this allowed Rosie, on occasion, to take advantage. Rosie could also be heard on a regular basis shouting at Elsie, the kitchen maid, if the breakfast trays weren't ready or properly set. Elsie very rarely left the kitchen and looked worn out most of the time, her complexion pasty with dark shadows under her eyes. The cap she wore was obviously too big as it was forever falling over her forehead. She rarely had much to say and just seemed to accept her lot in life with no ambition to move on from being at Mrs Mead's beck and call.

Mrs Mead had worked at the manor house for over thirty years. During that time, she had seen the master and Lady Emily grow up, numerous household changes and staff come and go. She ran her kitchen with military precision; Elsie's repeated sloppiness was a sure way to ruffle Mrs Mead's feathers. Her time was precious, and she didn't suffer fools gladly. In addition to the vast quantities of food she prepared and cooked on a daily basis, a multitude of tasks weighed heavy on her time. These included checking produce from the estate garden and farm, placing orders with the butcher, planning the menus with Her Ladyship and stocktaking with Mrs Harvey.

Martha's first month in service had been a steep learning curve with many errors made, and at times there had been tears. Working downstairs was an intricate system of precise organisation overseen by Mr Hampton and Mrs

Harvey. Everybody worked hard—except the footmen, or so it seemed to Martha. They carried meals to and from the dining room, polished the silver, waited at the dinner table, filled the coal buckets and looked dashing in their livery. When there were guests at the manor house, either Charlie or Arthur would stand duty in the hall. There appeared to be plenty of time for them to read the newspaper in the servants' hall or have a smoke in the courtyard.

"You ready, Martha?" Rosie called from the hallway.

"Yes, ready to start the day," she said, closing the door.

The two maids walked down the stairs and collected their housemaid's boxes. It was time to begin their work for the day, which would be the same tomorrow, and the day after, and all the days after that.

Chapter 2

November came quickly, and Martha's attic room had become incredibly cold. It was so much harder to get out of bed on a bleak November morning, but Martha forced herself out from under the blankets.

"Hello, Charlie. Why do you look so miserable?" she asked, as the footman passed her on the stairs without acknowledging her.

He kept on walking.

"What's the matter with him?" she asked Nell.

"He was hoping to have been offered the new under butler position, but Mr Hampton has employed a new member of staff, so Charlie's not very happy," Nell whispered.

"Oh, I see," Martha replied and made her way to the drawing room.

It was one of those days when all the rooms had to be turned out. The three maids, armed with their boxes brimming with cleaning supplies, began their tiring and laborious tasks.

Later that afternoon, the servants were introduced to Edgar Cuthbertson, the new under butler. He was shorter than both footmen and carried a little more weight. His hair was thinning slightly, which made it difficult to put an age on him. He was smartly dressed in a light brown suit, white shirt and brown tie, and looked very uncomfortable standing in the doorway, clutching his small, battered brown suitcase.

"Hello, everybody, it's nice to meet you all. I would prefer to be called Ed, if that is all right," he said, turning to Mr Hampton for his approval.

Instantly, Charlie snatched up the newspaper and walked out of the servant's hall without acknowledging the new member of staff.

"Come on, lad, let's get you some food; you must be frozen," Mrs Mead said, while desperately trying to tuck her rebellious wiry hair back under her cap. "Leave your case there and follow me to the kitchen."

She does like to feed us all up, thought Martha.

Charlie was sitting outside in the penetrating cold of the courtyard. Even from the back, there was an air of anger about him.

Rosie briefly stopped by to talk to him when she returned from the village, before making her way indoors.

"Far too wintry to be chatting outside," she muttered as she made her way to stand by the fire. "He could be just as miserable inside where it's warm."

For the next couple of days, a tense atmosphere lingered in the servant's hall. Everybody made a conscious effort to make Ed feel welcome, trying to compensate for Charlie's continued rudeness. None of this had gone unnoticed by Mr Hampton. He promptly gave Charlie a warning, making it abundantly clear that he needed to buck his ideas up or there would be consequences.

The little chat seemed to do the trick. Whether he wanted to or not, Charlie's attitude towards Ed did change, and the servant's hall was a much happier place for it.

The following morning, Mrs Harvey summoned Martha, Rosie and Nell to her parlour.

"Master William is returning, so we need to open up his room and prepare for his arrival," she announced, sounding quite excited.

Rosie and Nell looked shocked, but Martha knew nothing about the master—only that he didn't reside at the manor house.

"Right, come along, girls—he will be arriving by lunchtime tomorrow." She guided the maids out of her room then headed towards the kitchen to discuss with Mrs Mead the preparations for the master's long-awaited return.

"Well, that's a turn up for the books, after three years away," Rosie commented.

"Why did he leave?" asked Martha.

"Long story, haven't got time now."

Nell didn't comment. She just collected her house-maid's box and set about her work.

There was a lot of chatter at mealtime that night, and eventually, Martha was told the reason why Master William had left the manor house. Charlie did the honours; Martha listened attentively, not wanting to miss anything.

"Well," began Charlie, "Master William was engaged to Lady Amelia Southwick, bit of a catch for her money but not much to look at."

"That's not fair—I thought she was quite pretty," Nell said.

Charlie rolled his eyes, sat back in the chair and continued. "Anyway, not long after the engagement, Lady Amelia found out she was expecting," he said with a grin on his face.

"Expecting what?" asked Martha.

This caused a loud outburst of laughter, making Martha, at just sixteen, suddenly feel very naïve.

Charlie gestured a pregnant belly.

"Oh, oh I see," she said, her cheeks turning pink with embarrassment.

"Now, this is where it gets interesting. Master William was not the father of the child, and Lady Amelia would not divulge who the father was." He looked straight at Martha when he spoke, which made her cheeks glow even more.

"As you can imagine, upstairs were not happy and neither were the Southwicks. Master William broke off the engagement.

"Shortly after, Lady Amelia was found floating in the lake at the bottom of the estate. Rumours were rife that Master William had drowned his fiancée. However, the inquest confirmed that she had taken her own life. Master William was unable to cope with all the gossip and accusations, so he left to live with relatives in Scotland, and that's where he's been until now." Charlie stood up and took a bow. Martha had found his storytelling enthralling and had been hanging on his every word.

"We'll have no more gossiping if you don't mind, especially as the master will be back tomorrow," announced Mrs Harvey, waving her arms in the air to disperse the little crowd huddled around the fire.

There was much anticipation the following morning. At midday, the staff were requested to be present for the master's arrival. The two footmen, head butler, under butler, housekeeper and both lady's maids formed a line at the front of the manor house to welcome him home. Martha was eager to witness his return. She made her way to the top of the stairs and pushed the door that led into the great entrance hall slightly ajar. It was just enough to view the family. Lord and Lady Leatherby and Lady Emily were waiting to greet Master William. She couldn't quite see his arrival at the front of the house, but she was able to view the family as they walked back into the entrance hall accompanied by the master.

Both women looked stylish and elegant. Martha was in awe of Lady Emily. She wore an elegant, pale lilac, full-length dress with a round neckline and three-quarter sleeves. An ivory sash sat just below the bust line, which emphasised her petite frame. Her shiny chestnut hair was beautifully pinned away from her face and decorated with an ivory and gold comb. The hairstyle complemented her delicate features perfectly.

Her Ladyship, slightly shorter than her daughter, looked sophisticated in a slim, pale grey skirt, accompanied by a white full-sleeved, high-neck blouse. Around her waist sat a black satin sash. Her greying hair was quite severely styled, but a number of loose tendrils were left to frame her unlined face.

His Lordship was smartly dressed in a dark grey suit, white shirt and grey tie. He was quite handsome, with greying hair and a neatly trimmed moustache. Master William was shorter and much thinner in the face than his father, sporting thick black hair that was groomed to perfection. His face was kind, gentle looking.

Suddenly there was a hand on Martha's shoulder. She was spun around to find herself facing Mrs Harvey. She had been so engrossed in the homecoming events, all track of time had been lost. Mrs Harvey didn't have to say a word; just a glare was required to spark an apology from Martha, which came flooding out while she promptly made her way back downstairs.

There was an air of excitement throughout the household at the return of Master William. Mrs Mead and Elsie were in a frenzy making sure the welcome home food, both luncheon and evening dinner, was the best they could possibly serve. Luncheon was light, but the evening dinner was to be a true celebration feast to welcome the master home.

Gradually, everything began to wind down. The footmen served the family their late supper, and the bedroom candles were handed to any member of the family who wished to retire. Arthur helped Mr Hampton lock up the house, and Elsie made a final check that the kitchen fires were safe. The last duty of the day was to take the hot water bottles to the family bedrooms.

It had been an interesting day. After all, it's not every day there is a homecoming.

Chapter 3

Martha had not seen her family since her arrival at the manor house in September; it was now the first week of December. She would dearly love to see them all before Christmas, and she thought about home while walking towards the village on an errand for Mrs Harvey.

Her father and brother were miners, and her younger sister was still at school. At 4 a.m., the long walk to the pit would begin. When their shift finished, both men arrived home at 4 p.m. exhausted and covered in coal dust with only the whites of their eyes showing. In front of the fire, the tin bath would always be waiting for them, filled with hot water from an endless amount of kettles.

They lived in a small miner's cottage at the end of a row of eight. It had just two bedrooms, which meant Martha had needed to share with her sister and brother. Downstairs there was a kitchen and a front room. The kitchen was dominated by the copper, a large, cauldron-shaped tub that was built into the kitchen and used to wash clothes. Monday morning was always wash day. Martha's mother would tirelessly fill the copper with water and light a fire underneath to heat the water. Beating the clothes in the tub and then squeezing them through the heavy old mangle was a backbreaking and time-consuming task. If it wasn't possible to hang the clothes outside, they were hung on lines strung across the kitchen.

Martha sighed, realising how much she missed her everyday life with her family. Her thoughts of home were broken as she approached the village and the wonderful Christmas decorations came into view, commanding all her attention. There were wreaths on every door and cosy, inviting shops full of glittering Christmas gifts. She posted the letters she had been given and began her walk back to the manor house.

The winter sun was low, casting a glaring brightness across the sky. The severe frost from the night before hadn't melted, and the bare branches glistened in the sunlight.

"Morning, lass," said Albie.

"Hello, Albie. It's a lovely morning. Looks as if you've been very busy, collecting supplies ready for the Christmas wreaths." She nodded to his wheelbarrow piled high with holly and mistletoe.

"Here, have some, lass—a bit of Christmas cheer for your little room." Albie handed Martha a small bunch of holly.

"That's very kind of you, Albie. We always have holly in a vase at home; it will remind me of Christmas with my family."

She thanked him again for his kindness and set off up the path.

She was relieved to arrive back at the house and stand in front of the roaring fire; she was cold to the bone. Mrs Mead had spotted her carrying the bunch of holly and gave her an empty jam jar.

"Here we are, lass. That's all I got, but it will hold water just the same as any vase will."

"Thank you, Mrs Mead. Now it will be Christmas in my room!" Martha said as she rushed to put the holly in water.

During the afternoon, the family had announced they would be travelling to London the following morning with the intention of staying for two nights. Muriel and Ethel were required to travel with Her Ladyship and Lady Emily, and Ed would be required as His Lordship's valet. Master William, however, had chosen not to join the rest of the family and would remain at the manor.

Mr Hampton and Mrs Harvey decided it would be a favourable time to allow the housemaids the opportunity to visit their families before Christmas. It was decided they should leave after lunch, stay overnight with their loved ones and return the following day. This ensured they would all be back on duty well before the family's return.

Mrs Harvey announced the good news to the three girls. Martha and Nell were ecstatic at the thought of spending time with their families. Rosie, however, showed no emotion and certainly no excitement. Unlike the other two girls, Rosie never spoke of her family, and Martha and Nell didn't feel it was right to ask questions; they thought it best not to pry. She politely thanked Mrs Harvey, turned and walked out of the room.

"Here you are, lasses. A little present to take home with you, and a Merry Christmas to your families," said Mrs Mead, handing both girls a jar of homemade plum jam. The jam looked delicious, and the little jar appeared very festive, with a small piece of cream linen placed over the top held in place by a thin red ribbon.

"Thank you so much," said Martha.

"Yes, thank you, Mrs Mead," added Nell.

That night, Martha was convinced she would never be able to sleep; she was so excited. But sleep came to her quickly, as it always did. The following morning, she woke feeling joyous instantly remembering that after lunch, her journey home would begin. There was a real spring in her step as she dressed for the day ahead. From the window, she could see the dazzling white, frosty fields in the distance. Her small room had a raw feel; it was so bitter she could see her breath and the water in the jug on the dressing table was icy cold, but none of that mattered. She was going home.

When she collected her housemaid's box, she noticed that Nell had already taken hers, but Rosie's was still where she had left it the day before.

"Mrs Harvey, where's Rosie?" she asked, concerned.

"In bed, lass," answered Mrs Mead before Mrs Harvey had a chance to reply.

"Yes, thank you, Mrs Mead, and you're quite right—Rosie is unwell and has taken to her bed," Mrs Harvey said, taking control of the conversation. "We can't afford to have illness spread downstairs, and heaven help us should it spread to the family, so Rosie will eat in her room until she has recovered. Mrs Mead, please arrange for Elsie to lay a tray for her."

When the morning work was completed, Martha darted to her room, taking the stairs two at a time. She collected her hat and coat, not forgetting the jar of plum jam. She walked with Nell as far as the village, then they went their separate ways, both giddy with excitement at the thought of seeing their families.

***

Rosie had woken that morning feeling as if she were under a black cloud. She'd hated the thought of seeing Martha and Nell so happy at the chance to go home and made her way downstairs before the two girls were up and about. As she did, she pinched both her cheeks to redden them.

"Good gracious, girl, you look as if you have a fever," said Mrs Harvey as soon as Rosie entered the room.

That was the exact response she had hoped for. Rosie confirmed that she felt unwell, and Mrs Harvey instantly dismissed her, emphasising that she must stay in bed away from the rest of the household. Rosie hastily returned to her room. Lying in bed, she struggled to feel comfortable, weighed down by the guilt for her lie. She started to think about her family and the reason why she had never visited them in all the time she had been working at the manor house.

Whenever she thought about her family, she felt sad. At the age of fourteen, there had been a horrific pit disaster close to where she lived. She could still hear the deafening roar of the explosion followed by the sight of the soaring flames. Rosie had run to the scene of the explosion, holding her younger brother's hand, her mother following close behind. Her father and older brother had both left for the pit that morning. Men rushed to the rescue, frantically attempting to remove the wreckage. There was a sense of urgency and blind panic. These men weren't trained at rescue; they were endangering their own lives trying to save others. It was an almost impossible task—there was no way of knowing exactly where the miners were trapped.

The rescue attempt continued throughout the night and the following day and the days after that. After twenty-one long hours, the first survivors emerged from the mangled pit until eventually fifty-one men were pulled free. The women of the village had kept vigil at the pit, waiting anxiously, desperately hoping that the next survivor out of the wreckage would be their man.

But for Rosie's mam, it didn't happen. There were 149 men in the pit when the explosion took place. Only fifty one survived. Rosie's father and brother weren't among the lucky ones. Her brother was just sixteen years of age; he lost his life, along with twelve other young men, all under the age of twenty-one. It took seven days to recover all the bodies, and every day was heartbreaking. Loved ones grew emotionally drained and grief-stricken.

The tally lad who performed the daily tally checks for each shift knew every miner who had entered the pit that day. Mercifully, he made the identifications. Rosie's mother was devastated but was relieved that she didn't have to endure the agonising task of identifying the bodies of her husband and son. She would be forever grateful to the young tally lad who saved her the torment.

The house had felt empty and silent with Rosie's father and brother gone. There was no longer a wage coming in, and with three mouths to feed Rosie's mother had to find work. She was forced to take in home-based work so she could earn a wage and still look after her two children. Rosie had to take responsibility for household tasks, while her mother took in laundry and worked at finishing garments for a local factory. They grew their own vegetables and kept chickens. It was difficult at first. Rosie missed her father dreadfully and longed to hear her brother's banter. But the three of them settled into a routine, and life gradually started to return to normal, until Rosie's mam announced that she was getting married.

It had been just one year since the pit disaster, and Rosie couldn't accept that her mother wanted to remarry so soon. Stan was introduced into the household; Rosie took an instant dislike to him. But the wedding went ahead, and soon, three became four.

Stan was also a miner. He had never married and had remained at home with his mother, who had spent her entire life pandering to his every request. When she passed away, he married Rosie's mam soon after.

Daily life changed for the two siblings. Stan expected his new wife to continue with her work of finishing garments and taking in laundry, as well as tending to his every need. He demanded his breakfast on the table, and there would be hell to pay if the tin bath wasn't filled with hot water and his clean clothes were not waiting for him by the time he returned home from the pit. He would drink far more than he should, something Rosie's father had never done. Stan headed for the pub every evening after his tea. Some Monday mornings he was too drunk to attend work after using his Friday payday to drink excessively right through the weekend. When he returned home from the pub, he was loud, abusive and demanding of Rosie's mother.

Rosie and her brother loathed him. They despised being in his presence. There was a change in Rosie's mother; she became nervous—scared, even. She was exhausted trying to maintain her paid work and being at her husband's beck and call.

Stan arrived home from the pit one day, and Rosie's mother had lost track of time with the amount of work she'd had to finish. As a result, the tin bath wasn't full, and his clean clothes hadn't been ironed. His temper was vile. He lunged for Rosie's mam and swiped her so hard across the face she reeled to the floor. Rosie ran to help, but quick as lightning, he grabbed her by the hair and dragged her across the stone floor. He flung her out of the door into the back yard. Taking off his belt, he thrashed her again and again.

Rosie didn't make a sound. He was a large, muscular man, and to struggle would have been futile; the outcome would have been far worse. She gritted her teeth through every brutal blow. Finally, he let go of her, and she dropped to the floor.

Her mother had attempted to get up, but the strike to her face had been so fierce it had knocked her dizzy. Stan seized her mother by the arm and led her to the tin bath, demanding she fill it.

Rosie knew she could no longer live with this monster, and that night, when he had passed out from an overload of beer, she left. She was just fifteen.

She spent two days walking to get as far away from her unhappy home-life as possible, sleeping in a run-down barn one night and under the stars the second. The balmy night air was filled with the powerful scent of wild summer flowers, and the cloudless sky boasted stars that sparkled in all their glory. During those two days, she had relished her freedom, but she needed work. She had approached numerous stately homes and manor houses, enquiring if there were any vacancies. Time after time, she was refused, until she'd arrived at Leatherby Manor.

When she entered the courtyard, it was such a hot afternoon Mrs Mead was standing in the doorway fanning herself with a hankie.

"Can I help you, lass?" she asked, in between huffing and puffing.

"I was wondering if you have any work. I don't mind what I do," Rosie asked, sounding enthusiastic, working hard to hide how despondent she felt. She had been refused so many times.

"Well, now. I'll call Mrs Harvey—she's the housekeeper and the best person to ask about work." Mrs Mead quickly turned around and walked back into the servants' quarter, still fanning her shiny red face.

Mrs Harvey appeared and Rosie repeated her question.

"As it happens, we are a housemaid short, and I haven't placed the advert yet."

Mrs Harvey beckoned her in and, after a short chat in the housekeeper's parlour, agreed to take Rosie on as a housemaid on a trial period. That was three years ago. She hadn't ventured home since.

Chapter 4

The anticipation of seeing her family began to overwhelm Martha. It was dark and bitterly cold, but as soon as she turned the corner, she was filled with warmth at the sight of the little miner's cottage. The air was crisp, and Jack Frost was already beginning to make an appearance. A welcoming candle glowed in the downstairs window of every cottage, boasting an amber shimmer of light. Grey smoke made swirling and winding trails from the chimneys. Martha began to speed up until soon she was running. Before entering the cottage, she peered through the front window. The blazing fire looked so inviting. Her father was sat in his comfy armchair wearing his newly washed and ironed clothes, not a black pit mark to be seen, her little sister contentedly perched on his lap. Her mother walked in carrying a steaming mug of tea.

"Well, if it isn't our Martha!" shouted a voice from behind her.

Before she had a chance to answer, she was scooped up and swung around in a big bear hug.

"Tommy, put me down! I'll be dizzy," she protested.

"Aren't you glad to see your big brother?"

"Of course I am; I've missed you all."

"Well, come on, let's get inside." He caught hold of her hand and pushed the front door open.

From the tiny entrance, Tommy shouted. "Mam, Dad, look who I found on the doorstep!"

He opened the door that led into the front room and stepped inside, pulling Martha behind him.

"Well, if it isn't our Martha! You look fine, lass, you really do," her father said, pride written all over his face.

"Mam, it's our Martha come to see us!" shouted Tommy.

Her younger sister leapt off her father's lap, and in her excitement, she tripped over the rug and landed at Martha's feet. She jumped up at once and placed both arms around Martha's waist, squeezing as tightly as her little arms would allow.

Martha smiled up at her mother, who was watching almost warily, as if she could not believe what she was seeing. A beaming smile gradually spread across her face, creasing the corners of her eyes, and Martha knew that her mother, too, had missed this closeness with every beat of her heart.

"Hello, Mam. I've wanted to see you all so much," Martha said as they hugged each other.

It felt good to be back in the little cottage. Martha beamed with happiness.

"What you got there, lass?" asked her dad, looking at the package in Martha's hand.

"It's a jar of plum jam. Mrs Mead—she's the cook—gave it to me and told me to tell you all to have a Merry Christmas."

"Well now, that is kind. You be sure to say thank you, lass," her father insisted.

They all sat in the cosy front room, listening intently as Martha gave a detailed account of life in the manor house. Outside, it was fiercely cold, but the fire crackled and radiated its warmth through the little miner's cottage. It was a far cry from the elaborate rooms at Leatherby Manor. There were two comfy armchairs side by side, one looking slightly more threadbare than the other. The patterned wallpaper that once adorned the walls had been painted an uninteresting mustard colour. Hanging from the picture rail on one side of the room was a wedding photo. Martha had loved this picture for as long as she could remember; her parents looked so young and in love. On the opposite side of the room hung a happy family photograph.

There was a square table in the centre of the room with four hard-back chairs. One padded cushion seat was missing, and the remaining three were biscuit thin. Draped over the table was a crimson chenille cloth with fringes. This was the table covering that only saw the light of day at Christmas; it always made an appearance on December 1st, adding a touch of much-needed colour to the room. Carefully placed in the centre was a vase of holly proudly displaying an abundance of shiny red berries.

A candle burned brilliantly in the front window, and there were two smaller candles on either end of the mantelpiece. Beneath the table sat a large, faded rug, covering the majority of the stone floor.

Martha felt content and grateful to be spending time with her family and relished every moment, but all too soon, it was time for bed. Her sister, Tilly, slept all night tightly wrapped around her big sister. She was enthralled by every detail of Martha's new life and wouldn't leave her side.

***

The movements of her father and brother preparing for the long, bracing walk to the pit stirred Martha. She gently moved Tilly, trying her best not to disturb the little girl, and went to say goodbye to them both.

"Bye Dad, bye Tommy," she said, hugging each of them in turn.

"You take care now, lass," her father said. He turned away sharply, but not fast enough to hide the glistening in his eyes from Martha. Her heart seized.

Tommy hugged his sister and kissed her on the forehead, then followed his dad out of the front door. Tears stung Martha's eyes, threatening to escape any moment. It would probably be spring before she saw them again.

After the two men had left, Martha found her mother in the kitchen. It was warm and cosy, and she was grateful to have the opportunity to be just the two of them. Tilly was still asleep, so they talked, ate breakfast and enjoyed each other's company; she had missed these special moments. Martha told her mother that having holly in her room made her happy, it triggered so many joyous memories of home, but Mrs Mead only had a jam jar for her to put it in.

"A jam jar! We can't have that, love," her mother said, walking towards the larder in search of something better.

She returned with a small vase. "Here we are, love. It's very old and has a chip in the rim, so be careful; you don't want to cut yourself."

"Oh, Mam, this is so much nicer than a jam jar." Martha got up to give her mother a big hug.

Tilly wanted Martha to walk her to school. She had loved having her big sister home, even if it was only for one night. At the school gates, Martha gave Tilly a hug and wiped away the tears that were flowing freely.

Tilly walked backwards across the yard, waving until she was unable to wave any longer, then turned around and disappeared through the school door. Martha quickly made her way home; soon, it would be time to begin her journey back to the manor. The sky was a sea of blue. There wasn't a cloud in sight, and the sun was beaming, but there was no heat, just an icy chill and the grimy smell of chimney smoke. The ground was frozen solid—Jack Frost had certainly done his job overnight—and it didn't look as though it was going to thaw that day. She pulled at her hat, dug her hands deeper into the pockets of her coat and hurried back to the cottage. There was a welcome mug of hot tea waiting for her.

"Here you are, love, this is for you. Merry Christmas," her mother said, planting a kiss on her daughter's cheek and handing her a Christmas present.

"What is it?"

Her mother laughed. "Well, open it! That way you'll find out."

Martha pulled at the string and unwrapped the brown paper and saw what was inside. "Mam, I need these so badly. Thank you." She flung her arms around her mother, not wanting to let go because when she did, she knew she was going to have to leave.

Reluctantly, she put her hat and coat on and picked up the dark green mittens her mother had knitted for her. They were just the perfect present. After another big hug, she started her journey back to the manor house.

"Martha! Martha! You forgot your vase!" her mother shouted, flinging her shawl around her shoulders and running after her daughter.

"Oh, Mam, what would Mrs Harvey have said when I asked her if I could go back home to collect my vase?" Martha laughed.

Her mother stood and waved. Martha's heart ached to think of her heading back inside, alone, to continue with the daily chores.

Martha walked swiftly to ward off the painfully cold wintriness. The ground was so frozen it was uneven to walk on. Her feet began to hurt with every solid freezing mound of earth she felt through the soles of her shoes. As the afternoon started to lose its light, the bare branches of the trees were silhouetted against the clear sky, giving an eerie appearance. The temperatures were falling even lower.

Martha arrived at Packhorse Bridge, which indicated approximately another half an hour's walk. The instant she stepped onto the bridge, she recalled the game she had played as a child with her father whenever they crossed a bridge. She leaned over the side to listen to and watch the water gushing below. She snapped off a twig and let it drop into the water, then moved to the opposite side of the bridge to watch the twig emerge from under the arch below her. In the winter, they'd dropped twigs, and in the summer, they'd dropped leaves. Such lovely childhood memories.

Without warning, she was grabbed from behind and dragged across the bridge. Once she was off the bridge, the culprit tried to force her to the ground. Martha fought with every muscle in her body. She raised her arm, and with as much force as she could muster, she struck the attacker on the side of the forehead with the glass vase. He promptly let her go, stumbled and dropped to the ground.

She was rigid with shock, transfixed by the blood seeping from a gash on his temple where the vase had struck. He started to stir and tried to lift himself off the ground but quickly fell backwards, then there was no movement. Martha couldn't tell if he was unconscious or if the unthinkable had happened and he was dead. Grasped in a fit of panic, she hurled the vase into the undergrowth and started to run, but in the frenzy of the situation, she took the wrong route. When she realised that she didn't recognise any landmarks, it dawned on her that she was lost. She sat down to catch her breath, having no idea what to do next.

"Are you all right, young lady? Do you need any help?"

Martha looked up. In her confusion, she hadn't heard the horse approaching.

"I'm lost, sir," she replied, hurriedly trying to wipe her teary eyes. "I need to get back to Leatherby Manor; I work there."

"And I live there," the gentleman said, leaning over for her to take hold of his hand.

As she did, he pulled her up, and before she knew it, she was on the back of his horse. Then, like a bolt of lightning, she recalled where she had seen his face before. It was Master William.

"Hold tight!" he shouted.

Martha felt strangely comfortable and protected riding with Master William, her arms firmly around his waist. What would Mrs Harvey have to say about this?

The ride to the manor house was no longer than ten minutes. When they arrived, Master William helped her down.

"Thank you, sir," Martha said, trying hard to smooth her ruffled coat and straighten her hat.

"You're welcome. Your name is?"

"Martha, sir. I'm one of the housemaids, sir."

"Well, Martha, if I were you, I would make your way inside to warm yourself up."

"Yes, sir, I will, sir, thank you."

Master William led his horse off to the stables, and Martha ran through the courtyard and into the house.

"Good gracious, lass, you look as if you've been dragged through a hedge backwards," exclaimed Mrs Mead as Martha almost knocked her over in her haste to find Mrs Harvey.

She banged on her parlour door. Once inside, she broke down into floods of tears, and it took a considerable amount of time for her to recount the story in between sobs.

"Did you inform the master about the attack?" Mrs Harvey asked.

"No, I just said I was lost, then I told you straight away, like you and Mr Hampton always tell us we must do," Martha replied. With her voice breaking and her hands shaking, she wiped her tear-stained face with the back of her hand.

"Well, thank goodness for that. So let me see if I have got this right before I speak to Mr Hampton. You think you may have killed a man with a glass vase because he attacked you. Then, while you were running away, you got lost and had a ride home on the back of the master's horse," Mrs Harvey reiterated clearly and slowly with a look of shocked horror on her face.

"Yes, yes, that's right. It was on the Packhorse Bridge, but he is lying by the bridge, dead, I'm sure—there was blood and everything. The vase had a chip in the rim so it was sharp; it must have caused the blood and..." Martha's voice was rising, becoming high-pitched and quick.

"You must try to calm down, Martha. Wait here—I'm going to find Mr Hampton." Mrs Harvey gently pressed on her shoulder so she would sit down.

On Mrs Harvey's return, accompanied by Mr Hampton, Martha was a little calmer and was able to give a more detailed and coherent account of what had happened. The next step was to inform Master William.

Mrs Mead did what she did best and arranged a hot drink and some food. Martha couldn't stomach the food, but the drink was welcome.

***

Mr Hampton hastily made his way upstairs. Before entering the drawing room, he straightened his tie and took a deep breath.

"Sorry to disturb you, sir. It's about the young housemaid you—"

"Martha?"

"Yes, sir."

"What about her, Hampton?"

"She was attacked, sir, before you came across her."

Hampton recounted the full incident. Appalled by what he was told, William immediately arranged for two stable lads to ride across to Packhorse Bridge and investigate. On their return, they reported that the culprit was no longer at the bridge. He was obviously not dead and appeared to have made his escape. The important thing was Martha was safe and well; therefore, William didn't deem it necessary to take the matter any further.

However, he intended to discuss it with his father on his return from London.

Mr Hampton was informed, and in turn, he relayed the outcome to Martha.

"But there was blood, and he wasn't moving and…"

"He was probably knocked unconscious, and as soon as he came around, he got up and ran off for fear of being caught. Not for you to be worrying about now," advised Mr Hampton. "The best thing you can do is forget it happened."

Slowly nodding her head, Martha made her way to her room. Due to the circumstances, she was excused from her evening duties. Relieved to be crawling into bed, she hoped she would soon forget the whole upsetting incident. Well, maybe not all of it. She had quite enjoyed the ride back with the master.

Chapter 5

When Martha woke the following morning, she focused immediately on the holly in the jam jar, remembering why it was still in the jar and not the little chipped vase. Jumping out of bed, she walked to the window. Although the attic room was biting cold, the view always softened the blow. It had snowed lightly overnight, and a perfect white blanket veiled the usually lush green fields. She was mesmerised by its beauty.

Dressing quickly, she nimbly pinned her auburn hair into a small bun which sat neatly just above the nape of her neck, threw some stone-cold water over her face, tied her shoelaces and headed for the door.

"Martha, are you ready?" Rosie called.

"Yes, just," she replied.

She hadn't seen Rosie the previous evening.

"Are you feeling better?" she asked when they met on the stairs.

"Yes, much better, thank you."

Before Martha could ask her any more, Rosie changed the subject.

"Is it true you were riding the master's horse?" she asked, sounding as if she hardly believed she was saying such a thing.

"Well, I wasn't riding it by myself, Rosie. I had to hold on to the master or I would have toppled off."

"Bloomin' heck, Martha. I bet Mrs Harvey had something to say about that."

"I think she was too shocked. You should have seen her face!"

"I hope you said thank you."

"Yes, of course I did. He's the master—it wouldn't do not to say thank you, would it?" Martha laughed, passing Rosie her housemaid's box.

Mrs Harvey called the two girls into her room and announced, "Nell didn't return yesterday, so I am sorry to say there will be extra work for you both."

Before either of them could question her, she took hold of each girl by the shoulder and encouraged them out of the room, closing the door behind them.

***

After weeks of longing to be warm and cosy in the farmhouse where she had grown up, enjoying supper with her family, Nell was elated when she was given the time to visit them. Living on the farm had been a way of life for her father since he was a young boy. The tenancy had been passed to him when her granddad had died. Nell knew keeping the farm in the family was paramount to him, but she had no desire to spend her working life on Apple Tree Farm. For as long as she could remember, her dream had been to become a housemaid in a big house.

Nell's father had been bitterly disappointed when she announced her intentions to leave the farm to work at Leatherby Manor. From a very young age, they had been inseparable. Even when her two sisters had arrived, it was always Nell who pulled at his heartstrings, so when he displayed a profound anger at her decision, she was deeply hurt and upset.

As the day to leave the farm had grown closer, her father started to distance himself from her. The atmosphere in the farmhouse was dire, and eventually, it became intolerable. Nervously, Nell had approached her father about the festering situation; his personality had altered so much she hardly recognised him. Sitting side by side, he touchingly explained the reason for his behaviour. The thought of not seeing his beloved daughter every day was unbearable; it filled him with dread. He realised it was a selfish attitude, but he didn't know how to let her go, so he'd distanced himself from her, which he'd assumed would prepare him emotionally for when she was no longer around.

By the time Nell left for Leatherby Manor, bridges had been built and the closeness they had enjoyed since she was a little girl rekindled. Deep down, her father knew farming was not right for his daughter, and Nell left the farm with his blessing.

With all her heart, Nell was convinced she had made the right decision, especially when she remembered how much she had detested the farming chores assigned to her—especially daily egg collection.

Nell held enormous respect for her mother and how tirelessly she worked. Being a farmer's wife was unrelenting. Keeping on top of everyday household chores, farm duties and milking was demanding. Nell had been truly grateful that she'd never been assigned as a milking helper. Thankfully, that had fallen to one of the farmhand's children.

There was, however, one chore Nell had taken great delight in. She'd never failed to enjoy delivering the freshly churned butter to the local shop. Old Mrs Thirsk would allow her to choose either two bull's eye sweets or a piece of toffee from the tray of homemade toffee she religiously displayed on the counter. Nell would watch in fascination as she smashed it into unevenly shaped segments with a small silver hammer. The aroma of the sweet, sticky caramel toffee was heavenly; it was always her first choice.

There were countless memories of playing in the broken haystacks, repeatedly climbing to the top of the stacks then sliding back down. Her two younger sisters were not old enough to contribute to the running of the farm, but they eagerly joined in the haystack fun. All three of them would return to the farmhouse covered in straw, harbouring insects, which had made a home for themselves in the comfy stacks.

Now, as she walked through the frost-covered fields towards Apple Tree Farm, Nell could see the church spire. Reunion was less than twenty minutes away. She climbed over the last stile and crossed the field towards the farm. The light had almost faded, but she could still distinguish the silhouette of the farmhouse with a welcoming glow in the downstairs window guiding her like a beacon. She would be home before it became completely dark. As she got closer, familiar smells greeted her. The most pungent was that of the dairy. The sour smell lingered in the air, a true indication she was home.

She opened the farmhouse door, which led directly into the kitchen. The scene inside mimicked a traditional Christmas card. Her father was seated in a battered old armchair, tapping his pipe on the wooden arm with the newspaper sprawled across his lap. Her mother was about to lift the blackened kettle off the hearth, and both her sisters were sitting cross-legged on the stone floor in front of the roaring fire surrounded by Christmas paper chains, lovingly made to decorate the farmhouse. Dodger, the black-and-white Border Collie, heard the latch click on the door. He bounded across the kitchen from under the table, greeting Nell with a shiny wet nose and an overload of sloppy kisses.

"Hello, Mam. Hello, Dad."

She stood in the doorway, waiting for their response.

"Oh, my love, it's so good to see you," exclaimed her mother as she replaced the kettle and greeted her with open arms.

"Well that it is, lass, that it is." Her father did not move from his armchair but patted the seat of the chair next to him, beckoning his daughter to sit down. "You need something warm inside you, love."

Her mother promptly organised a steaming bowl of broth and a chunk of homemade bread.

"There now. Eat up."

She felt content and warm, safely embraced by the homely cheerfulness of the farmhouse. That night, she slept soundly and was shocked to find it was light when she woke. Her sisters had already left on their journey to school, and her father was out on the farm. As she made her way downstairs, the smell of sizzling bacon wafted to greet her.

"Mam, you let me sleep so long."

"They must be working you too hard in that big house. You needed a good night's rest," her mother replied as she placed a sturdy farmhouse breakfast with homemade bread on the table.

Nell devoured it, not realising how ravenous she was.

"I'm just going to find Dad, then I'll be on my way back to the manor house."

"Take this with you, love," her mother said.

"Still forgetting his lunchbox then, is he?" Nell laughed as her mother handed her the forgotten box.

Her mother rolled her eyes and shook her head. "Never changes, does your dad."

The fields had frozen overnight, and even the duck pond was iced over well enough to use as a skating rink. It all looked magical in the golden morning sunshine, but it was bone-chillingly cold. Nell turned the collar up on her coat and rubbed her hands together to keep them warm. In the distance, Dodger was romping across the vast, frozen field towards her.

"Hello, Dodger, good boy, Dodger. Where's Dad then, where's Dad?"

She followed Dodger but was unable to keep up as he ran ahead. As she approached the lower field, she began to call to her father. There was no reply, and he was nowhere to be seen. She climbed over the frosty stile into the next field and there in the corner, lying on the ice-covered earth, she saw him.

Sheer panic engulfed her, and she ran frantically across the field. Dodger was still sprinting ahead of her.

"Dad! Dad!"

But he didn't reply.

By the time she reached him, Dodger was lying by his side, licking his face. She dropped the lunchbox and knelt down on the solid wintery ground.

"Dad, it's me, Nell. Open your eyes, Dad, you've got to get up."

Utter terror took hold. It gripped her tight and strangled the edges of her words. She took her coat off and laid it across his chest. He was so cold.

"Dad!" she shouted, shaking him. There was no response.

"Dad, wake up. Dad, please."

Tears began to trickle down her cheeks at the realisation her father was dead.

She knew she had to get help, but at the same time, she didn't want to leave him on his own in the frosted field.

"Stay, Dodger, stay!"

Her command was stern and full of authority. Dodger took up his position sitting alongside his master. Wiping the tears from her eyes, she found herself running at speed across the fields back to the farmhouse.

Halfway across, she saw Seth, the farmhand.

"Lass, what on earth is wrong?" he asked, seeing how distressed she was.

"It's Dad. He's... I think he's..." She was breathless but striving to express the urgency.

"Where, lass? Where is he?"

"The bottom field, he's in the bottom field."

She watched Seth race away, but in her heart, she knew it was too late.

When she reached the farmhouse, her mother was in the yard feeding the chickens.

"Nell, where's your coat, love? You must be frozen to the bone."

"Mam, you need to come in."

"Your voice is so serious, Nell. What's wrong?"

The rest of the day passed in a blur of disbelief. Nell walked to the village school to collect Violet and Lizzie. Her father's body was brought back to the farmhouse, and one of the farmhand's children was sent with a message to the undertaker. Only when the shell of a temporary coffin was brought to the house did the tragic events of the day begin to sink in. Her two sisters found it difficult to comprehend that they wouldn't see their father again. Her mother was in shock; she simply sat in the armchair next to the fire. Not crying, not talking, just staring. Nell had taken charge. Her grief was all-consuming, but she had to remain in control. Realising it would be impossible for her to leave the farm and return to the manor house, with a heavy heart and tears streaming, she wrote a letter addressed to Mrs Harvey and placed the envelope in her pocket, knowing it would need to be sent first thing the following morning.

Chapter 6

Although the weather had turned much colder, Martha and Rosie were in the courtyard enjoying the winter sunshine and fresh air, sitting side by side on Charlie's wooden smoking crate. Mrs Harvey flung the door open and stood at the top of the steps.

"There you are! Master William wishes to speak with you, Martha. Make your way upstairs. Mr Hampton is waiting for you."

It was hard to tell which of the girls looked the most shocked.

"Me, Mrs Harvey?" Martha said, not sure she had heard correctly.

"Yes you, Martha. Hurry now, run along."

She bolted up the stairs, flung open the door and arrived in the entrance hall breathless and red-faced. Mr Hampton was standing outside the drawing room, beckoning her.

"Oh my goodness, girl, you look like an overripe tomato; I don't know what the Master will think—and straighten your cap. Remember, only speak when you are spoken to." The warning was delivered with stern authority.

As they entered the drawing room, Master William walked towards them. "Very well, Hampton," he said, and signalled for him to leave. "Hello, Martha."

"Hello, sir," she replied tentatively. She felt uncomfortable in the drawing room with a member of the family; it went against everything she had been taught.

"Hampton informed me of the attack you suffered. Have you recovered from the shock, and are you well?" His voice was soft, and he sounded genuinely concerned.

"I am, sir. Very well, sir."

"I'm pleased to hear that. As you know, when the stable lads returned from Packhorse Bridge, there was nothing to report. We can only assume the culprit, although injured, managed to make his escape. Mrs Harvey tells me you were returning from a visit to see your family at the time the attack took place."

"Yes, sir. I was, sir."

Momentarily, she forgot Mr Hampton's warning only to speak when you are spoken to, and before she could stop herself, she started recounting her visit home. Realising the error of her ways, she became flustered.

"Sorry, sir, I didn't mean to…"

"Not at all, Martha. It made interesting listening. I would enjoy a visit there one day, providing your family wouldn't object."

"No, sir. They wouldn't, sir."

At that point, the drawing room door opened, and Mr Hampton announced luncheon.

William collected his newspaper and slipped it under his arm. "Good day, Martha. I'm glad you are well," he said, which was a signal for her to leave the drawing room.

"Good day to you too, sir," she replied politely and promptly left the room.

As she crossed the hall, she failed to notice William glance back at her before he entered the dining room.

She scurried back to her duties, not quite believing what had just taken place.

"Back with the workers now, I see," Charlie teased as she entered the servants' hall.

Much to her annoyance, her cheeks became noticeably flushed.

"You like the master, don't you?" He laughed, giving her a nod and a wink.

"Stop teasing the lass," scorned Mrs Mead, standing in the doorway, hands on hips.

"I think he's a nice man," Martha replied defensively as she walked past Charlie, who was wearing a big grin on his face.

Martha had difficulty drifting off to sleep that night, which was not usually the case. She found herself recalling the events in the drawing room. She tossed and turned until eventually, she succumbed.

***

The following morning brought the arrival of Nell's letter addressed to Mrs Harvey.

"Oh dear," she said out loud as she read the awful news.

Then her role as housekeeper took over and reality struck: it was very close to Christmas and the household was now a maid short. It would be impossible to enrol a new maid before the festive season; the earliest would be in the new year. Despondent, she gathered all the servants together to deliver the sorrowful news about Nell.

Martha was fond of Nell, and a wave of sadness flooded over her at the thought of not seeing her friend again. Then she immediately felt guilty for thinking about herself before Nell. After all, the reason she was unable to return was due to her father passing away. Martha's mind raced, and she thought of her own father, shuddering at the idea of ever losing him.

Preparations for Christmas continued, and there was much kerfuffle below stairs. Christmas was approaching fast, and there was an innumerable amount of organising required. Mrs Mead was methodical and precise, which would ensure that Christmas Day flowed without a hitch. She was the sole keeper of the larder and prided herself on it being fully stocked with game from the shoot, a plentiful supply of vegetables, meat and dairy from the manor farm, and the essential Christmas hamper orders had been placed with Harrods and Fortnum and Mason. She was a force to be reckoned with, and the family were more than willing to overlook any flaws and shortcomings of hers. They were a small price to pay to be served delicious food daily, without fail.

"It's arrived then," announced Charlie, entering the servants' hall and picking up the newspaper as he walked past the dresser.

"What's arrived?" Martha asked.

"The Christmas tree. Must be twenty-foot tall, lying on the floor of the great entrance hall, waiting to go up."

Martha was suddenly overcome with excitement at the thought of seeing the decorated tree. It would bear little resemblance to the sprigs of holly that were displayed in her parents' modest cottage. Nevertheless, it was a sign that Christmas was drawing closer, and Martha adored everything about Christmas.

When she'd wake on Christmas Day, she would gingerly reach for her stocking (one of her father's old socks), which had been hung at the bottom of her bed. She remembered the suspense she felt, not knowing if the stocking would contain the much longed for orange, apple and nuts.

The three siblings would always receive a toy, also placed in their stockings, the nature of which would depend on how much her parents had been able to afford that year. Her favourite Christmas present ever was the year she received a baby doll. She loved it the moment she set eyes on it. The doll became known as Sally. Sally had the brightest blue eyes, rosy apple cheeks painted on her delicate porcelain face, and wispy blonde hair that poked out from underneath a pink and white bonnet. The bonnet and cardigan had been lovingly knitted by Martha's grandmother. There were pink ribbons instead of buttons on the cardigan and matching ribbons to tie the bonnet. The doll was second hand, but the newly knitted set of clothes had given it a new lease of life. Sally became Martha's constant companion.

Martha always delighted in the build-up to Christmas Day and dearly loved Christmas Eve. There was so much busyness and lots of last-minute shopping. She recalled the local butcher shouting loudly to passersby, trying to sell all his stock before the meat turned. Carol singing and present wrapping with her brother and sister. The gathering of all the ingredients to make the Christmas pudding. The most exciting detail of that was the tradition of placing a polished three-penny bit into the mix. The three children would take turns to stir the pudding for luck before the mixture was placed into a china bowl then boiled in a large pan for up to eight hours. It was Martha's job to keep a close eye on the water and inform her mother when the pan needed to be topped up. This was an important job as she was preventing the pan from boiling dry and protecting the precious Christmas pudding. Only once had she had the good fortune to find the coin. It had jarred her tooth badly, but she was overjoyed it was she who had found the three-penny bit.

The job of preparing the turkey for cooking was horrific. The birds were sold with their feathers, heads and innards intact. Her father would take the bird into the back yard to remove all the unnecessary bits. Everybody stayed inside until the deed was done. Handling the bird outside kept the house clean and prevented the tiny feathers finding their way up your nose.

Martha felt downcast at the thought of all the Christmas festivities that she held so dear continuing without her.

"Stop daydreaming—we have work to do," shouted Rosie.

The two housemaids had been asked to collect an endless supply of boxes that were brimming with Christmas decorations. By the time they arrived in the entrance hall, Albie the gardener and two of the farmhands were making hard work of trying to stand the twenty-foot tree upright.

"No, lads, over a bit. That's it, lads, that's it!" shouted Albie. "No, a bit more, lads. Stop, STOP!" He sounded exhausted with all the to-ing and fro-ing.

Albie had been employed on the estate since leaving school over fifty years ago. He lived alone in a small cottage on the edge of the estate. His wife, Maud, had died four years earlier. They had longed for a family but were never blessed, so Maud had poured all the love she had for children into volunteering at the local school. As Albie was a much-valued member of staff at Leatherby, arrangements had been made by the family for him to remain in the cottage after his retirement until the end of his days.

The monstrous tree had to be manoeuvred into position so that it was in line with the gallery that surrounded the hall. As head gardener, it was Albie, who had to commit to the confirmation that the tree was straight. This took him a little while. First, he put his glasses on, and then, he viewed the tree with his glasses off. Then he stood at the far side of the hall, and lastly in the middle of the hall. Everybody held their breath for fear the towering tree would need to be moved... Eventually, the confirmation came.

"Job done," he said with a look of satisfaction on his face.

A huge sigh of relief was let out by everyone.

Martha and Rosie were given the tedious job of fixing the candle holders to the branches: the next step in the many stages of decorating the mammoth tree.

"How do we reach the top branches?" Martha asked as she leaned her head back to take in the height of the tree.

"A ladder, lass. The only way is a ladder," Albie declared, stepping back and letting out a long whistle while he mopped his brow.

"Shall we start?" Rosie said, unenthusiastically beginning to drag the boxes closer to the tree.

"I would much prefer to dress the tree with all those beautiful baubles," Martha said, pointing at the box containing a multitude of delicate glass balls, but that privilege fell to the lady of the house.

As far as the two girls could reach, they painstakingly fixed the candle holders. Albie secured the ladder, making it safe enough for Martha to climb so she could attach the remaining holders further up while Rosie supervised their positioning.

Some considerable time later, the holders were complete. Next, the candles had to be placed into them. It was a tiresome job that neither housemaid enjoyed. The Christmas tree was now ready for Her Ladyship to dress.

Two days later, after the family had finished their evening meal, the entire household was invited to the great hall to view the magnificently decorated Christmas tree.

"Everybody upstairs quickly, quickly," shouted Mr Hampton. "Let's not keep His Lordship waiting."

Charlie and Arthur were already in the hall. With great caution, they had laboriously lit every candle in readiness for the viewing.

Martha was beside herself with excitement; she could hardly wait to view the tree. The housemaids, the kitchen maid and Mrs Mead were the last servants to arrive, and the scene that greeted them took Martha's breath away. The tree, which two days earlier had looked bare and forlorn lying on the floor, now looked spectacular. Every candle flame burnt robustly, casting a golden shadow across the intricate glass baubles. Ruby red velvet bows were scattered regally amongst the branches. Sitting with pride at the top of the tree was an angel. Her shimmering gold wings shone in all their glory amongst the flickering of the candles. It was perfection. Martha was speechless; she had never seen such a wondrous sight.

The banisters that led to the gallery were adorned in lush green garlands and ivory lace bows complemented by large, deep red velvet bows attached to each spindle.

She was so dazzled by the decorations she failed to notice the family. Standing alongside Lord and Lady Leatherby were Lady Emily and Master William. His

Lordship thanked his wife for the splendid decorating of the tree, and thanks were given for everybody's hard work which had resulted in a superb display.

It was time for Martha to return to her duties, but before doing so she kept the door leading downstairs to the servants' hall slightly ajar. She stole one last peek at the sheer beauty of the Christmas tree, only to feel the flush in her cheeks as Master William spotted her and waved. She abruptly closed the door and dashed downstairs, willing her glowing cheeks to subside.

Chapter 7

The next couple of days passed in a frenzy of Christmas organising. There were a hundred and one things that needed to be done, and the advert for a new housemaid had slipped Mrs Harvey's mind.

"Rosie, I need you to take this card to Mr Withers and ask if he would kindly place the advert in his shop window," she said, sounding fraught.

"But Mrs Harvey, the weather…"

"No buts. Rosie, you will be there and back before you know it. Hurry, before Mr Withers closes the shop." She handed Rosie the advert, turned and walked away, giving her no further room to protest.

Rosie popped the card into the pocket of her tunic, donned her hat and coat and reluctantly made her way to the village. The wind raged through the trees, and the heavy grey clouds raced across the sky. The afternoon light was gradually fading.

I most certainly won't make it back before dark, she thought, struggling to protect herself from the continual gusts of wind.

There was a stream of busy Christmas shoppers weaving in and out of the colourful shops, but the festiveness of the village passed her by. She was too cold and too miserable to take any interest. Arriving at Mr Withers' shop was a welcome relief from the elements, and the cosiness inside melted her miserable mood slightly.

"Mr Withers, could you place this advert in your window for Mrs Harvey please?" She struggled to remove the card from her tunic pocket; her hands were so cold.

"Yes, of course, lass. Something hot to warm you before you start trekking up that hill?" Mr Withers asked. He shook his head and pursed his lips in sympathy at Rosie's frozen appearance.

The sky was darkening outside, but Rosie found herself nodding eagerly when asked if she would like a mug of hot chocolate. She took a chair in the corner of the shop and waited for Mr Withers to return with the steaming mug of loveliness.

"This will warm you, lass," he said and passed it to her.

It was the most delicious hot chocolate she had ever tasted—so much so she didn't want it to end.

"Thank you, Mr Withers," she shouted and left the shop to begin her struggle back to the house in what felt like a gale-force wind.

It was now dark, and the gusts were unforgiving. She quickened her pace, all the time thinking of the roaring fire and how she longed to stand in front of its heat.

Due to the rustle of the swirling leaves and the howl of the wind through the bare trees, she was not aware of the man following her until he lunged from behind and hurled her to the ground. He swiftly dragged her away from the path. She tried to scream, but her assailant flung himself on top of her and brought his hand down fiercely to cover her mouth. She was repulsed at the stale smell of tobacco and whiskey. With every breath in her body, she courageously tried to fight him off, but he was unrelenting and took what he wanted. She felt an excruciating pain and then nothing; she passed out. Her attacker raced from the scene, leaving Rosie unconscious and violated.

When she came to, Rosie had no inclination as to how long she had been lying unconscious on the cold, damp ground. She was rigid with terror and afraid to move, fearful that the monster who had raped her was still nearby. Eventually, when she was certain he had fled, she dragged herself up and continued her walk to the house. It was difficult to focus; her vision had become distorted as the tears flowed uncontrollably.

"They can't know what's happened; I don't want them to know what's happened," she said out loud, placing one painful foot in front of the other.

Her whole body ached. Aware that her tunic and undergarments were torn, a feeling of shame washed over her.

The lights of the house came into view. She prayed the dinner gong had sounded and the preparations for the evening meal were in full swing. This would allow her to enter the servants' quarters and run directly up the stairs without anybody noticing her. It was a tall order, but it could be done.

She walked across the courtyard and cautiously opened the door. As suspected, there wasn't a soul in sight. Everybody was busy. Mrs Mead could be heard barking orders at Elsie from the kitchen, and voices echoed from Mr Hampton's pantry. Without stopping to close the door, Rosie dashed up the stairs and into her room. She collapsed onto the bed, sobbing and shaking violently.

***

"Martha, have you seen Rosie? She should have been back by now," asked Mrs Harvey as she paced back and forth between the kitchen and the servants' hall.

"No, Mrs Harvey, not since she left for the village."

Martha was beginning to get concerned. There was no reason why Rosie's errand should have taken so long.

***

Upstairs, Rosie removed her tainted clothes, flinching as she touched them. Her cheek was scratched, and her elbow was bleeding as a result of being thrown so forcefully to the ground. She poured water into a bowl and bathed both injuries. Changing into her second uniform, she re-pinned her hair and made her way downstairs. Her stained clothes needed to be taken to the laundry; the repairs she could take care of on their return.

Just as she was about to enter the laundry room, Mrs Harvey made an appearance.

"What took you so long, Rosie? And what have you got there?"

"It's my uniform, Mrs Harvey. It was dark and I fell and..."

"Are you hurt?" Mrs Harvey asked, sounding concerned.

"Just a scratch, and my tunic is torn," she replied, not looking directly at Mrs Harvey.

"That can be dealt with, don't worry. On with your work, now—Martha is run ragged; she'll be glad to see you back."

Mrs Harvey took the bundle of clothes off Rosie and placed them in the laundry room.

***

When Martha caught up with Rosie, she was instantly aware something was wrong.

"What happened to you?" she asked worriedly, pointing to the scratch on Rosie's cheek.

"It was dark, I was rushing to get back and I fell. I'm all right—nothing to worry about." Rosie turned away from Martha as she spoke, making an extra effort to tidy her housemaid's box.

"Well, you don't look all right to me. Are you sure you're well?" Martha asked again.

"I said yes, didn't I?" shouted Rosie abruptly, and she started up the stairs, away from Martha.

It was 10 p.m. and both girls had finished for the night. Martha climbed the stairs behind Rosie, they said their good nights, but Martha was troubled. She was certain there was something wrong.

***

A biting cold Christmas Eve dawned, and Martha's room felt the iciest it ever had. Yearning for the warmth of the fire, she dressed hurriedly and was glad to hear Rosie call.

"Coming!" she shouted.

The fire was as welcome a sight as she had imagined. There was just enough time to enjoy the heat of the flames before she had to begin her duties.

"Today is going to be a busy day," Mrs Harvey announced in her sternest of voices. "Lady Emily's young man and his parents, Lord and Lady Enson, will be arriving for dinner. I will be performing the finger test when you have completed your dusting, and I shall expect to find all rooms spotless."

Mr Hampton was busy planning the wine list, after which he intended to prepare the silver and glassware, ready for the evening festivities. He would leave no stone unturned, priding himself in delivering the best service possible.

Mrs Mead was in the throes of preparing the menu, which had been discussed with Her Ladyship weeks before. Everybody knew to stay out of the kitchen unless it was an emergency of magnitudinous proportions. There would be no mincing of words from Mrs Mead if you dared to get in her way—nobody wanted to be in that line of fire.

Unfortunately, the household was down to just one footman; Arthur was confined to his bed with a fever. He had taken advantage of his afternoon off the previous day but had felt unwell on his return. Mr Hampton had promptly banished him to his room. Ed had been assigned to assist Charlie, not that he would be very much help. As an under butler, he wasn't familiar with the duties of a footman.

Rosie and Martha worked in silence. Usually, the two girls shared some banter but not today. Rosie wanted to keep herself to herself, which highlighted to Martha that all was not well. She didn't push the issue and hoped Rosie would confide in her when the time was right.

"There will be an announcement this Christmas, just you mark my words," said Ethel as she sauntered into the servants' hall.

Charlie peered over the top of his newspaper. "Announcement about what?" Even though he was the only footman at present, he still managed to flaunt plenty of free time. He looked quite content with his feet up, reading the paper.

"An engagement, of course." Ethel sighed, sounding as if Charlie should have known what she was referring to. "Lady Emily has all the latest fashions to wear this Christmas. I'm telling you—there will be a wedding in the house by the summer, you just wait and see." She nodded as she spoke, then turned and made her way upstairs to assist Lady Emily.

"Will there now? And since when did she become a clairvoyant? And anyway, I thought Ethel said she hadn't seen lover boy for a while, so how would she know about an engagement announcement? Too nosey for her own good, that one," Charlie said, returning to his newspaper.

Ethel Brooks was the house gossip; she liked to think she knew everything that was going on upstairs and downstairs. Discretion should have been a key quality for any lady's maid, but Ethel lacked it sorely. You could count on her to keep everybody informed of Lady Emily's suitors. Charlie had very little time for it, but Martha enjoyed listening to her accounts of Lady Emily's life, particularly when she detailed the outfits she wore to various functions. It was a world away from anything Martha had ever known.

Before retiring for the night, Martha and some of the other servants spent time preparing the servants' hall for Christmas lunch the following day. Coloured paper chains were placed along the walls and diagonally across the ceiling. Taper candles were displayed in heavy brass holders with a circular base. A large, bulbous (or in Charlie's words, ugly) green vase painted with over-sized white flowers held a vibrant bunch of holly, courtesy of Albie. Mrs Mead had made it very clear that the holly was not to obstruct the framed picture of the king and queen. As a result, it was placed off centre on the mantel-piece, which pleased Mrs Mead but irritated Mrs Harvey. Mistletoe tied with deep red ribbon hung from the centre of the room.

Much to Mrs Mead's disapproval, the holly wreath used as the table centrepiece made its appearance again. It had seen better days, but unfortunately, Mrs Harvey in-sisted the battered decoration made its debut every year. The once cheerful red flowers looked tatty and faded. The green foliage had discoloured, and there were nu-merous gaps where ribbons and bows should have been. The brilliant white tablecloth was a stark contrast to the shabby, tired-looking centrepiece. Christmas crackers were placed at every setting, and a woollen sock was hung on each chair. It was Mrs Harvey's job to fill the stockings. Every member of staff was awarded a small gift wrapped and labelled by Her Ladyship. This was a tradition that all the staff appreciated.

That evening, Rosie excused herself with a headache and didn't stay to help. Martha, Charlie and Elsie did the best they could to cheer up the dreary room. When they had finished, Mrs Mead whipped them up a steam-ing mug of hot chocolate each. In double-quick time, Charlie flipped open a hip flask and poured some of the contents into his hot chocolate.

"Charlie, what have you got there?" Martha asked, straining to see into his mug.

"Nothing for little girls," he laughed and covered the top of the mug with his hand.

"I'll have you know I am not a little girl—I will be seventeen this coming year—and it smells like whiskey to me, Charlie Ackworth," was Martha's cheeky reply.

"I give in then. You're not a little girl, and yes, it is whiskey, but don't you go telling," he said, winking at the two girls.

Ed had missed out on all the fun of decorating. Charlie had left him on hall duty, in charge of collecting the coats for the departing guests and arranging for the cars to be brought around to the front of the house. Considering they had got off to a bad start, Charlie and Ed now appeared to be quite good friends. Very often they were seen in the courtyard together enjoying a smoke and on occasion a little drop of something.

Charlie and the two girls spent a while longer gathered around the cosy fire enjoying the calm before the Christmas Day mayhem. Then, one by one, they retired for the night. Mrs Mead remained in the kitchen, mulling and fussing over Christmas lunch, and poor Ed was still on hall duty as it appeared that none of the guests were making any attempt to leave despite the late hour.

***

Martha woke to her first Christmas day without her family.

"Happy Christmas, Mam. Happy Christmas, Dad. Happy Christmas, Tommy and Tilly," she said out loud, then leapt out of bed, dressed and was ready for the day ahead.

"Merry Christmas, Rosie. How are you feeling today? Is your headache better?" she asked, as the girls made their way along the corridor.

"Merry Christmas, Martha. I'm all right," she replied, but there was a disturbing emptiness in the tone of her voice.

Christmas Day was the one day of the year that the family served themselves at luncheon. Mrs Mead prepared a cold buffet, and the footmen arranged the food in the dining room, after which the entire family would retire to the drawing room to open their Christmas presents. This allowed the staff time to enjoy their much-deserved Christmas lunch undisturbed.

At 1 p.m. precisely, Mr Hampton expected everyone to be seated in anticipation of lunch being served. Charlie and Arthur, who was now fighting fit, placed themselves in charge of the crackers, ensuring there were no escapees; all silly hats must be worn. Charlie being Charlie took centre stage and read all the cracker jokes. The atmosphere was jovial and full of festive cheer; even Mr Hampton looked to be relaxed and enjoying himself. However, he did seem to be having difficulty with his paper hat. It appeared smaller than everybody else's, and it sat balancing precariously on the top of his head.

Martha's eyes almost popped out of her head when she saw Mrs Mead carrying a tray displaying a hog's head stuffed with sausage meat and a rosy red apple in its mouth. Elsie followed close behind with a tray of cold meat. The main course consisted of a joint of roast beef accompanied by Yorkshire pudding and a variety of vegetables. The "pièce de résistance" was the Christmas pudding. The magnificent plum pudding, bathed in brandy and set alight, was a sight to behold. It was a feast for a king, Ed announced. They raised their glasses to a toast: "Mrs Mead!" they all echoed.

"Oh, away with you all," she said, secretly loving every minute of the glory.

Martha opened her present from Rosie and was touched; it was such a thoughtful gift.

"Thank you so much."

"You do like it, don't you?" asked Rosie.

It was a little glass vase, second hand but pretty, to replace the one Martha had lost.

"Oh I do, Rosie, I really do," Martha replied, handing Rosie her Christmas present.

Martha had visited the second-hand shop and bought Rosie a pair of mittens, remembering how Rosie had admired the green mittens Martha's mother had knitted.

"Just what I really need!"

Rosie thanked Martha and tried the red mittens on for size. They were just perfect.

Both girls were grateful to receive a hairpin in their stockings as a gift from the family. The atmosphere in the servants' hall was jolly. The candles glowed, and the fire burnt brightly. Every one of the staff relished their free time and made the most of it by playing charades. Charlie won, of course. Then, at 6 p.m., the dressing gong sounded, and all too soon, their Christmas had ended and duty called.

By half-past ten, Martha and Rosie were exhausted. It had been a hectic day; their beds were calling.

"Good night, Rosie."

"Good night. Martha, I..." Then she stopped. "It's nothing. See you in the morning," she said, and disappeared into her room.

Martha wondered what she had been about to say. But she didn't ponder on it for too long, as within minutes of getting into bed, she was asleep.

***

"It's official: Lady Emily is to be married. There was a proposal last night, and she has accepted. Didn't I tell you? I did, didn't I!" Ethel proudly announced, looking very pleased with herself. She stood in the doorway to make sure everybody could hear.

"Well now, that is news indeed," said Mrs Harvey, though she didn't sound enthusiastic. Work downstairs would probably treble, Martha realised, if the wedding was to be in late spring or early summer.

The days between Christmas and New Year saw a constant throng of guests arriving and departing at the manor house. Two days before New Year's Eve, the servants' ball—an event the Leatherby family had advocated throughout the generations—was held in the servants' hall.

In preparation, the gramophone that normally resided in the drawing room was transported downstairs and placed with care by Ed on the dresser. He was noticeably relieved when it had been delivered safely. The trestle table was laden with party food; Mrs Mead had excelled herself once again. Uniforms were discarded, and the Sunday best came out in all its glory.

The ball commenced when Lord and Lady Leatherby took the first dance with Mrs Harvey and Mr Hampton. Martha was amazed at the elegance of Mrs Harvey dancing with His Lordship. She'd expected the family to remain for the duration of the ball; however, the procedure was for them to stay for approximately half an hour. After that, Charlie told her, the party would really begin.

"Would you like to dance, Martha?"

She recognised the voice instantly.

Standing to the side of her was Master William. The shock at his request left her struggling to find her voice.

"No, thank you, sir. I don't know how to dance, sir," she replied, feeling her cheeks flush pink, and wishing with all her heart that they wouldn't.

"It's not hard; just follow my lead." He gently pulled her towards him and slowly guided her to the music.

Her heart thudded in her chest. Her face was now noticeably flushed and if she didn't control her breathing, she feared she would faint.

When the music stopped, he thanked her and then returned to collect his drink.

"Enjoy the rest of your evening, everybody," announced Lord Leatherby, and the family made their way back upstairs.

"Well, lass, that was an honour, I must say," declared Mrs Mead. "Dancing with the master. Never seen such a thing, never."

She made short work of the sherry she was clutching. Martha caught Mr Hampton watching her with a frown as he poured himself a drink. She blushed and looked away. It was improper etiquette, she supposed, for the master to dance with a servant girl. Martha took a lot of teasing from the other servants, especially Charlie, who by the end of the evening was worse for wear, the culprit: whiskey.

Christmas is almost over, thought Martha, and although she hadn't been in a position to spend the time with her family, surprisingly, she had enjoyed her first Christmas at the manor.

Two days later, they celebrated New Year's Eve. The family served themselves drinks at midnight, allowing the staff time to revel in the New Year celebrations below stairs. Joining hands, they sang Auld Lang Syne and wished each other a happy and healthy new year.

Chapter 8

New Year's Day brought a howling, gale-force wind driving the heavy snow. Martha could barely see out of the window as patterned across the glass were delicate frosted designs, each one as intricate as the next.

Before beginning her day, she removed the holly from the vase Rosie had bought her. It was a new year, 1910, and her mam would never fail to pack away the Christmas decorations and discard the holly on January 1st. "Out with the old and in with the new", she would say. Staring at the empty vase, Martha thought how lovely it would look when it was filled with colourful spring flowers.

The new year had only just started, but preparations were well under way for Lady Emily's wedding. The date had been set for April 21st.

Downstairs, everybody continued with their daily chores, but Rosie's behaviour increasingly concerned Martha. Her personality had changed dramatically since the day she had run the errand to the village. She had become distant and withdrawn. The banter the two girls had shared was no longer present.

The scratch on Rosie's cheek had healed and so had the gash to her elbow, but inside, she felt torn apart. Every day, she prayed that the images of that fateful evening would leave her memory, but they never did; they had become engrained, and she felt increasingly more ashamed.

It was the second week of February, and there hadn't been one applicant for the empty housemaid position.

This was worrying; it needed to be chased up. Mrs Harvey added it to her list of things of things to do, which was becoming longer by the minute, and more urgent, too, with the wedding approaching so quickly. Mrs Mead was in full wedding mode, in complete control of the wedding breakfast and the baking of the all-important cake, which she had already started. She prided herself on the mixture, which was bejewelled with cherries and almonds, sultanas and grated lemon rind. Perfection was her intention; her plan was to rival the cake she had baked for Lady Emily's christening.

Mr Hampton had commenced his stocktake of the cellar in preparation for the vast amount of champagne and wine that would be consumed on the big day. This was a task of paramount importance and was taken extremely seriously.

The footmen were in charge of polishing the occasion silver and glassware. Arthur appreciated the importance of the assignment. Charlie, however, viewed it as an unnecessary task, failing to see that not just any silver or glassware would be fit for purpose as every item was cleaned or polished before storage. Needless to say, Arthur did the majority of the hard work.

Martha and Rosie were missing Nell. There were days when both girls fell into bed exhausted. Extra bedrooms were prepared in readiness for the guests who had been invited to stay at the manor house on the night of the wedding. Rooms were turned out and dusted from floor to ceiling with a thorough check performed by Mrs Harvey.

Life at the manor was frantic. As the wedding day drew closer, there was a definite air of anticipation and excitement.

Martha still tried to engage her friend in conversation, but a void had developed in their relationship, and she missed the old Rosie dreadfully. The other servants also noticed the dramatic change in her personality. Mrs

Harvey became increasingly worried and took steps to address the situation.

"You asked to see me, Mrs Harvey?"

"Yes, I did, come in, Rosie. I am concerned about you, are you not well?" Mrs Harvey asked her sympathetically. "You just don't seem to be yourself these days."

"Thank you for asking, Mrs Harvey, but I am quite well."

Rosie made every effort to disguise the sorrow in her voice, determined to make her reply sound convincing.

"Is there anything else troubling you?"

"No, Mrs Harvey. Can I go now?"

"Yes, Rosie, you can." She watched Rosie leave the room and shook her head, knowing deep down something was upsetting this young girl.

***

The weather was becoming warmer and the days longer. Spring was in the air. From her attic window, Martha watched the buds on the trees explode into leaf and the spring flowers begin to blossom. The field was overrun with playful lambs, all snowy white, apart from one black lamb who appeared to be the most playful.

The eve of the wedding had arrived, and the manor house was full of liveliness. Charlie and Arthur had been assigned to furniture removal, clearing space in the great hall for the wedding reception. Trestle tables were transported to their required position and covered in pristine white cloths edged in lace.

Martha and Rosie witnessed all the preparations as they hurried from room to room, checking and double-checking everything was in order before Mrs Harvey scrutinised their work.

The florist arrived to decorate the entrance hall, the staircase and the entrance to the manor. Martha had never seen so many flowers. The banister was decked in trailing ivy, intertwined with delicate cream roses and fragrant lily of the valley. Ivory lace bows were placed intermittently along the entire length of the winding banister. Pedestals of large cream roses, long-stem white lilies and a multitude of light and dark green foliage were placed at the entrance to the hall. Garlands of dainty white stephanotis were woven amongst the ivy and draped across the white tablecloths. Centre stage was the wedding cake, standing proud at four tiers high. Mrs Mead had lost sleep over her beloved cake on many a night; however, the result was spectacular. It was covered with ivory icing and piped to resemble delicate lace.

Martha watched as the finishing touch was added: a cascading display of flowers placed on the top tier. The combination of small cream tea roses and ivy added to the magnificence of the cake.

The last area to be decorated was the archway leading out of the great entrance hall. The ivy, roses and lily of the valley made a striking display, and the air was filled with a sweet, delicate fragrance.

Martha and Rosie had finished their duties upstairs and were making their way to the servants' hall when they were called to Mrs Harvey's room.

"I have scrutinised your work and performed the finger test."

The two maids held their breath.

"I have no complaints. Well done both of you," she said with a smile on her face.

Martha actually gasped and even Rosie couldn't keep the smile from her face—this was praise indeed.

The following day saw much pomp and ceremony. While the family attended the church service, the wedding breakfast was to be displayed ready for the guests' return. But before the start of the hard work, the staff were invited to view the wedding party leave the manor.

Martha watched wide-eyed as the bride made her appearance; she followed every graceful step Lady Emily made as she descended the ornate staircase. She looked a vision in her ivory bridal gown. The bodice was lace and extended to a high neckline. A narrow satin ribbon circled her tiny waist, below which a straight lace skirt fell effortlessly to the floor. The satin blouson sleeves were fastened at the cuff with a row of pearl and lace buttons. An elegant, floor-length veil was attached to a dazzling family tiara. Her long chestnut hair was loosely pinned, with fine curls left to frame her face. She carried a bouquet of cream tea roses and stephanotis, the symbol of marital happiness, and an abundance of trailing ivy. Martha had never seen anybody look so beautiful.

Lord Leatherby gently drew her veil to cover his daughter's face. She took her father's arm, and he proudly led her through the great entrance hall into the April sunshine.

Martha was brought back to reality, and the romance of the moment instantly disappeared as soon as Mrs Mead placed her hands on her shoulders and announced, "All hands on deck! We haven't got long before they are back and wanting feeding." She hurried the two housemaids and Elsie back downstairs.

There was a constant thoroughfare of servants up and down the stairs, carrying enormous amounts of food to the hungry wedding guests. Cold meats, mutton, pork, roast beef, plum pudding, duck, pheasant and a variety of cakes and tarts. Mr Hampton and Ed catered for the guests' every need; there was never an empty glass.

When the bride and groom were ready to make their departure to begin their honeymoon, everybody downstairs was invited to toast them and witness the bride throw her bouquet. The newly married couple glowed with happiness as they said their goodbyes. Lady Emily took her position on the grand staircase, turned her back and threw her bouquet, which was caught by her new sister-in-law.

That night, Martha lay in bed mulling over the events of the day until sleep got the better of her and she eventually drifted off.

***

"I just don't understand why we haven't had any applicants for the new housemaid's position, Mrs Mead—not one," complained Mrs Harvey as she entered the kitchen the following morning, shaking her head in disbelief.

"Rosie, could you make a journey to the village?" she asked, handing Rosie a much larger advert to be placed in Mr Withers' shop window.

Rosie hadn't ventured to the village since the attack and felt sick to the pit of her stomach at the thought of doing so, but she placed the advert in her tunic pocket and set off for the village. As she approached the spot where the attack had taken place, she stopped and started to tremble. The images were with her every day and every night, but the memories were so much more animated here. She was positive she could smell the whiskey and the staleness of tobacco. The tears flowed, and the trembling wouldn't subside.

She thrust the piece of card deeper into her pocket and ran back to the house. She didn't stop until she reached the servants' courtyard. To catch her breath, she sat on the steps, hoping with all her heart that none of the other servants would appear. When she was feeling calmer and more composed, she made her way inside.

"That was quick," exclaimed Mrs Harvey.

Rosie took her coat off and continued with her duties. She didn't have the energy to reply to Mrs Harvey; she just felt numb.

For almost four months, she had been carrying this dreadful secret. Although none of it had been her fault, she felt ashamed and worthless. She had deliberately distanced herself from the other members of staff and knew her change in behaviour had been a source of concern for everybody, but when asked if she was well, she could only assure the concerned person that there was nothing for them to worry about.

***

The mornings were getting lighter, and the birds were happily performing their morning song. It was a joy to wake up to, and Martha sprang out of bed, ready to face the day.

Rosie hadn't stopped to call for her, and as she had a little time before heading downstairs, Martha walked along the corridor and knocked on her friend's door.

"Rosie, hurry up—it's time we were downstairs."

There was no reply.

"Rosie, hurry up!" she shouted again, this time with more urgency.

There was still no reply.

Martha opened the door and burst into the room shouting, "Hurry up, Rosie."

And she stopped immediately, aghast at the sight which greeted her.

Rosie was slumped on the bed face down. A bottle of disinfectant lay on the floor beside the bed.

"Rosie? Rosie, please answer me, Rosie. Rosie!"

But there was no reply.

Martha turned and dashed from the room, leaving the door wide open.

She found Charlie and Arthur about to make their way to the dining room.

"You have to come now. You must come now—it's Rosie."

The urgency in Martha's voice unnerved both footmen, and they sprinted up the stairs.

Standing at the entrance to the room, they were open-mouthed at what they were witnessing. Arthur walked slowly towards the bed. Martha and Charlie stood in silence in the doorway.

Leaning towards Rosie, Arthur called her name, but there was no response. One of Rosie's arms was draped over the side of the bed. He attempted to find a pulse, but with a grim expression, let her wrist fall.

He tried again, this time Rosie's neck, but there was nothing.

"She's dead," he said softly, looking directly at Martha and Charlie.

Charlie didn't say a word. He just turned and left the room, making his way to find Mrs Harvey and Mr Hampton.

Martha stood transfixed, not believing what she was seeing. Her heart started to race. She could feel herself swaying, the colour drained from her tiny face. Arthur gently placed his arm around her shoulders. Then the tears came, slowly at first, until she had no control and she sobbed pitifully. Arthur guided her away from the room and closed the door behind them.

Chapter 9

Mr Hampton and Mrs Harvey arrived at Rosie's bedroom door. The housekeeper was hoping against hope that Charlie had been wrong. Mr Hampton cautiously turned the handle, and they both entered.

"Oh my goodness." Mrs Harvey gasped, raising her hands to her face.

Slowly, she walked towards Rosie's lifeless body. Mr Hampton remained at the door in disbelief. She gently lifted the young girl's arm. Turning to look at Mr Hampton, she simply shook her head.

"The poor girl," he said, closing his eyes and shaking his head rapidly as if trying to shake away the image he had witnessed.

"I asked her, I asked her if there was anything troubling her. I asked her more than once! The answer was always no."

"It's not your fault, Mrs Harvey. It isn't anybody's fault."

Mr Hampton removed a spare blanket from the shabby old wardrobe and, with great care, placed it over the body.

"We need to inform His Lordship and contact the girl's family," he said as he slowly walked away.

They left the room, not noticing an envelope which had been placed alongside the water jug and bowl.

***

Mrs Mead was deeply distressed by what she had been told but tried to remain calm and provided cups of tea for everybody. There was silence and disbelief in the servants' hall.

Charlie and Arthur were outside in the courtyard, both in as much shock as the others. They sat on two old crates, just staring straight ahead, not saying a word. Now and then, one of them would exhale a cloud of smoke, and periodically one of them would shake their head from side to side, unable to absorb the shocking sight they had discovered.

**

Mr Hampton and Mrs Harvey made their way upstairs to speak to His Lordship.

"Sorry to disturb you, Your Lordship. There is something you should be aware of. The housemaid Rosie is… She has… She's…"

Unable to bring himself to say the words, he trailed off, and Mrs Harvey took over.

"Dead. She's dead, Your Lordship. It looks as though she took her own life."

"Good gracious, Hampton. Do we know why? How? How did she commit suicide?"

"It would appear that she ingested disinfectant, Your Lordship," Mr Hampton said. "There was a bottle on the floor beside the body."

Pacing back and forth, Lord Leatherby thought for a moment, then said, "You will need to do all the necessary contacting, Hampton. Keep me informed. It's a tragic state of affairs, just tragic. How is everybody downstairs?"

"They are in complete shock, Your Lordship," Mrs Harvey said with sorrow in her voice.

On their return downstairs, Mr Hampton retreated to his pantry and started the sombre task of contacting Dr

Matthews and the undertaker. He obtained Rosie's home details from Mrs Harvey and was about to begin writing the solemn letter to her family when Lord Leatherby entered the room.

"I don't mean to disturb you, Hampton, but I think it best I speak to the girl's parents in person. We shall make the journey there first thing tomorrow morning."

"Very well, my lord."

Mr Hampton was relieved that he didn't have to compose such a tragic letter, but he didn't relish the thought of seeing Rosie's parents in person.

When the doctor arrived, Mr Hampton accompanied him to Rosie's room. Mr Hampton waited outside while Dr Matthews examined the body and retrieved the disinfectant bottle off the floor. It was while the doctor was washing his hands that he noticed the envelope. It wasn't addressed to anybody, therefore he decided that it should be handed to His Lordship.

"Thank you, Mr Hampton. I shall report my findings to Lord Leatherby."

Mr Hampton escorted Dr Matthews to the library.

"I have made an examination of the body, Your Lordship," Dr Matthews explained, "and it does appear that the girl swallowed a substantial amount of disinfectant; there were obvious signs of foaming at the mouth. During the examination, I also observed that the girl was with child. Approximately four months, I would say."

"Good grief, Matthews!" exclaimed Lord Leatherby.

"And there was this."

Dr Matthews handed His Lordship the envelope.

"Thank you, Matthews. Hampton will show you out."

Lord Leatherby poured himself a drink, sat at his writing desk and opened the envelope.

Not long after Mr Hampton had shown the doctor out did Lord Leatherby ring for him and Mrs Harvey. They found him in the library, staring distraught at the letter, which he silently pushed across the desk to them.

Rosie had poured her heart out in the letter. She described how ashamed she had felt since the attack. She had wanted to tell somebody but had been terrified of their response, fearful of what they would think of her. When she realised that she was going to have a child, she knew her fate was sealed. She was all too aware that it would entail instant dismissal the minute the pregnancy was discovered. There would be little opportunity for any further employment. Her shame and panic were clear in the words of the letter. The girl had seen no other way out.

Mrs Harvey and Mr Hampton were speechless at the revelation.

Lord Leatherby broke the heavy silence. "I shall take care of the funeral myself. The poor girl deserves as much."

***

The following morning, the sorrowful journey was made to inform Rosie's family of the tragic event. It was a beautiful warm, sunny spring morning, but the mood was subdued. There was very little conversation between Mr Hampton, the chauffeur and Lord Leatherby until they were a short distance from the mining village.

"This is the cottage, Your Lordship," confirmed the chauffeur.

Lord Leatherby studied the small miner's cottage. It looked so neglected and run down. Before leaving the car, he rehearsed in his head for the one-hundredth time how he was going to break the news to the girl's family.

The arrival of the chauffeur-driven car caused quite a stir in the small community. The children playing in the street rushed to huddle around the automobile, wondering at the rare sight. Mr Hampton and the chauffeur remained with the car and looked on as the children circled the vehicle in awe.

Lord Leatherby knocked on the door of the poverty-stricken cottage. There was no reply. He knocked again, and the door opened. Greeting him was a gaunt woman wearing what he could only describe as rags.

"Please excuse the intrusion," he said. "Are you Mrs Cummings, Rosie's mother? I am your daughter's employer, Lord Leatherby. Could I possibly come in?"

Rosie's mother didn't say a word. She just stood aside and beckoned Lord Leatherby in. The cottage was oppressive and smelt of smoke and stale cooking. She signalled to a seat, but he declined.

"I have news about your daughter. I am so very sorry to have to tell you, but she passed away yesterday."

There was silence. Rosie's mother didn't utter a word. There was no reaction, no display of emotion. Just silence.

"You do understand what I have just said, don't you?" Lord Leatherby's tone was soft.

He gently guided her to a chair. Placing his hands on her shoulders, he cajoled her to sit down.

At that point, the door to the front room was flung open. A red-faced man, Rosie's stepfather, launched himself into the room.

"And you are?" said the man in an aggressive tone.

"Good afternoon," Lord Leatherby managed to say, fighting to remain polite when faced with the hefty, scowling man. "I'm your daughter's employer. I have some bad news."

"I don't have a daughter," was the man's dismissive reply.

"Rosie, I have come about Rosie. Sadly, she passed away yesterday."

"It's her daughter." The man pointed viciously at his wife. "And good riddance, I say."

"Mrs Cummings, I—" Lord Leatherby began.

"She's Mrs Booth now. Cummings was the name of her old man before me. And don't think we can afford a funeral, because we can't," the man said, while attempting to light a cigarette.

"As Rosie's employer, I shall take full responsibility for the funeral. It will take place next week; you will be informed of the details."

"No need, we won't be going."

"But Mr Booth, it is—"

"I said we won't be going," Booth reiterated with venom in his voice.

Lord Leatherby glanced across at Rosie's mother. She hadn't spoken a word in all the time he had been there. He wasn't even sure she had fully taken on board the fact that her daughter was dead. He knelt down in front of her and touched her hand. She remained motionless, staring straight ahead.

"I am so very sorry for your loss," he said. "I really am."

There was no point continuing the conversation. He left the cottage and made his way towards the waiting car.

"Is there any money owing to the girl?" Booth shouted from the doorstep.

Lord Leatherby retraced his steps. "I would assume there is, yes. I shall ensure any amount owing will be forwarded to you."

"You do that!" Stan yelled, before slamming the cottage door.

Lord Leatherby couldn't comprehend the situation he had just been a part of. The hollow-cheeked, pitiful-looking woman was obviously terrified of her husband and had been mentally and no doubt physically abused, reducing her to a shell of a person.

"Hampton, please speak to Mrs Harvey on our return and request that any wages owing to the poor unfortunate girl be forwarded to her family as soon as possible."

***

The funeral of Rosie Cummings, aged just eighteen, took place five days later. There were no family members present. She had been let down in death as she had in life. It was attended only by Lord Leatherby, Mr Hampton and Master William.

The three men stood at the graveside in the torrential rain. It was a sorrowful sight. Rosie had deserved better.

Martha and the rest of the servants were finding it difficult to come to terms with her death. There hadn't been any banter or laughter in the servants' hall since that shocking day. Mrs Mead had done her utmost to cheer everybody up with lots of even more delicious food than usual, but there was very little enthusiasm, except maybe from Charlie. On the day of the funeral, the weather was dark and dreary. The rain was continual and showed no sign of letting up, which added to the gloomy mood inside the servants' hall.

"Hello, everybody. Why are there so many miserable faces?"

Standing in the doorway was Nell.

Chapter 10

"Is that Nell Robbins' voice I can hear?" asked Mrs Harvey, rushing into the servants' hall.

"Well, lass, it's nice to see you back, especially as Rosie has gone and there is..." shouted Mrs Mead from the kitchen, but she was quickly interrupted by Mrs Harvey.

"Come with me, Nell, and tell me how things are on the farm."

Nell picked up her bag and followed Mrs Harvey into her parlour.

"What did Mrs Mead mean when she said Rosie was gone?" Nell asked, having no indication of how tragic Mrs Harvey's reply would be.

She broke the news to Nell as gently as possible.

"Dead!" Nell exclaimed.

Mr Hampton and Mrs Harvey had decided there would be no point hiding any of the facts concerning Rosie's death. As sure as day follows night, the truth would find a way of surfacing regardless.

Nell was dumbfounded. Her first thoughts were of how unhappy and scared Rosie must have been and the sense of utter desperation she must have felt before making the heartbreaking decision to end her life.

A knock came at the door.

"Come in," shouted Mrs Harvey.

Mrs Mead entered carrying a tray with tea for two and a plate of warm scones.

"There you go, lass. You'll be needing these."

"It is good to see you back, Nell," Mrs Harvey said as she poured the tea. "Your room has remained empty. I advertised for a new housemaid, but there was not one applicant. Maybe it was meant to be."

After Nell's father's funeral, her life became challenging. It had been painful to watch her mother slip into oblivion; she became subdued and detached, losing interest in everything, including her two youngest daughters. Nell took responsibility for the household chores, farm duties and looking after her sisters' welfare. But it was the financial side that had worried her the most; she had very little knowledge regarding that area of the business, and it kept her awake at night. As much as she knew her duty was to remain on the farm, she'd longed to be back at the manor house. She missed the daily banter, even Charlie's cheeky and sometimes sarcastic remarks. From the day she had arrived at Leatherby Manor, she had taken pride in her work and genuinely appreciated her position as a housemaid.

At first, she'd been angry at the death of her father and being left with the demanding responsibility of the farm. It had weighed her down and felt like a millstone around her neck. She regularly cursed the farm, but the guilt she felt afterwards for her thoughts was agonising. What she really needed was time to grieve, but that was a luxury she could ill afford. There wasn't an hour or even a minute in the day for herself.

The farmhand, Seth, and his wife had been a great source of comfort. The family were caring, and she had welcomed their kindness. So, when Seth had approached her to discuss an idea he thought may help the situation, she was ecstatic.

"Can I have a word, lass?" he'd asked.

"Is there a problem?" Nell replied, crossing her fingers, hoping he wasn't about to give her any bad news.

"No problem, lass. It's just that me and the wife have been talking." Seth was standing with his hands in both pockets, casually leaning against the cowshed as he spoke. There was never any urgency with Seth. The only time Nell had witnessed him break into a sweat was the day he'd raced across the field to help her father. "We were wondering about what you would think if we took over the tenancy of the farm. You and your mam would have less responsibility, that's for sure. I know about the finances—I helped your dad many a time."

"Seth, that would be wonderful. You have no idea how worried I have been." Relief washed over her like the brightness of dawn.

"I'll speak with old Dawson, the landlord, and we'll get onto it straight away." Seth tipped his cap and strolled out of the barn.

Nell smiled for the first time in a long while, over-joyed. It was also the first time she had felt positive since the day her father had passed away.

The transferral of the tenancy had been agreed and Seth became the new tenant of Apple Tree Farm. With less re-sponsibility, it felt as if the millstone had been lifted. She'd finally had the opportunity to visit her father's grave, which gave her so much peace. It had taken gentle persuasion and patience from Nell, but eventually, her mother agreed to go. The quaint church with its immaculately maintained graveyard was situated at the far end of the village. The spring weather was perfect for walking, so they chose the route through the woods. The woodland floor was a sea of bluebells, and there was an array of wood anemones, their petite petals producing a white carpet of loveliness. The serene tranquillity was magical. Nell adored spending time in the company of nature and welcomed the calming effect it radiated.

Tentatively, Nell's mother had knelt at the grave and delicately placed a bunch of freshly picked woodland flow-ers. She took time to arrange the fragile blooms until she was happy with the display. Nell discreetly moved away from the grave, leaving her mother alone with her thoughts. She watched as her grief-stricken mother gently spoke to her husband. They had been inseparable since they were teenagers, and she had loved him dearly. He had been a good husband and a doting father. And now, he was gone.

"Nell, I'm ready to go home now," her mother called. Her voice sounded calm, and she had a look of contentment on her face. Nell hadn't seen her mother this composed since before her father had passed away.

They walked back in silent reflection until they reached the farm.

It was then that her mother hugged her, telling her it was time for her to return to Leatherby Manor. Nell realised her mother was ready to resume her duties on the farm, and without the responsibility of the tenancy, the load was lightened. But most importantly, Violet and Lizzie would have their mother back.

*****

The day after Rosie's funeral, the household resumed their normal duties, each and every one of them with a heavy heart. There was very little chit chat, and the woeful atmosphere hung in the air like a looming black cloud, felt by all.

"Come with me, Martha," Mrs Harvey said, taking Martha away from her work. "Constable Jennings is here to speak with you."

Confused, Martha followed her to her parlour, where the constable waited.

The attack on Martha had never been reported. Lord Leatherby had discussed the incident with his son but had decided there was little point taking the matter further, a decision he now bitterly regretted. He had tortured himself: would the poor housemaid still be alive if he had reported the first attack? However, the rape Rosie had suffered had been made known. Constable Jennings had shown great compassion and chosen not to speak with Martha until the upset in the household had subsided somewhat. He'd graciously waited until after Rosie's funeral.

"Nothing to worry about, lass," he told her. "We just need to know if you are able to give us any details about your attacker."

Constable Jennings had made himself comfortable in Mrs Harvey's armchair with his notepad at the ready.

Martha thought for a while.

"No, not really. It was getting dark, and it all happened so fast."

"Was he tall? Short? Thin, fat? Anything at all you can remember," the constable asked, his pencil poised.

"I can remember the blood. It was coming from the side of his forehead."

"And why would that be, lass?"

"I hit him with a vase that my mother gave me, Constable, and it had a chip on the rim."

Constable Jennings quickly entered the information into his notebook and was about to proceed with more questions when Martha suddenly remembered:

"There was a smell. Whiskey, I think, and the smell of cigarettes." She wrinkled her nose.

"And nothing else?"

"No, Constable, nothing," she replied, shaking her head.

"Well, that will be all for now, thank you, lass. If you remember anything, anything at all, you be sure to let me know."

Martha watched the constable leave and wished she could have helped him more. All he knew was that the attacker had smelt of whiskey and cigarettes, which covered more than half the male population of the county. Mr Hampton addressed the servants after their meal that evening. He made it crystal clear that the maids were not to visit the village on their own. If the errand was important then one of the footmen must accompany them. However, if there wasn't anybody available to take on the role of chaperone, the errand would have to wait.

His stern words left nervousness in the air. This person had attacked twice, and there was no evidence to suggest it wouldn't happen again.

Chapter 11

Nell settled back into routine very quickly. She and Martha were a good team. It was to remain just the two of them for the foreseeable future; everybody agreed it felt too soon to replace Rosie. However, it meant extra work for the two housemaids.

On May 6th, the household woke to the shocking news that the king was dead.

"Well, he didn't last very long," was Charlie's response to the news.

Edward VII had been on the throne for just nine years, just a fraction of his mother Queen Victoria's almost sixty-four-year reign.

Charlie walked across to the fireplace and removed the photo of the king and queen.

"So who's next then?" he asked.

Mr Hampton entered the room just in time to hear his flippant remark.

"Have some respect, lad. The poor man died of a heart attack, and he was suffering from pneumonia."

"George, his son, will be next on the throne," proclaimed Mrs Mead. "King George V and Queen Mary. God bless the king and queen." She was a staunch royalist, and woe betide anybody that had a bad word to say about the royal family.

The king's funeral was planned for May 20th. His Lordship and Master William intended to stay with family in London and witness the state funeral. Arthur and Charlie were required to accompany them as valets. Neither of the footmen had visited London previously, and they were obviously excited at the thought. Charlie more so than Arthur, which wasn't unexpected.

They commenced their journey to London the day before the funeral. On their arrival at Kings Cross Station, Lord Leatherby and Master William took a taxi to Belgrave Square, their residence for the next two days. Charlie and Arthur walked the four miles. Neither footman minded the walk as it gave them the opportunity to absorb the sights and sounds of London. The streets were lined with large, imposing buildings towering above the hectic streets. There was a wealth of shops with customers darting in and out at every opportunity. At Oxford Circus, a policeman was standing in the centre of the road directing the traffic. Horse-drawn carriages travelled alongside automobiles and open-top double-deck buses. The conductor was clearly visible on the packed top deck, ensuring every passenger paid their fare. Sandwich-board men in their white overalls and black caps walked the streets advertising anything from theatre matinee performances to hats from Paris and even automobiles.

"Do you think that number is right?" Charlie said, staring at the price of a motor car in disbelief.

Arthur thought for a moment. "Must be. No point them putting the wrong numbers up, is it?"

"No, I suppose not, but a hundred and fifteen pounds for an automobile!" Charlie shook his head.

They checked the directions given to them by His Lordship and decided they should get a move on. They had spent far too long enjoying the sights.

***

"George, William, it's so nice to see you both. We really don't spend enough time in each other's company. Come in, sit down. Watkins, please arrange some tea."

Charlotte, Lord Leatherby's sister, was pleased to receive such special guests. Her husband, Edward, had some business to attend to but would return in time for dinner. Charlotte was older than her brother and had married Edward at the age of nineteen, spending their married life residing in London, where she was actively involved in the London social scene. They'd developed an even busier social life after the tragic death of their daughter, Alice, at the age of just ten.

The family had been staying at their country home. Alice had relished the summer months they'd spent there, as the grounds gave her the freedom she didn't have in Belgrave Square. After the accident, the house was closed and it had never been reopened. Alice had fallen from a garden swing and hit her head with such force on the concrete edge of a nearby water feature she'd died instantly. Charlotte and Edward had never recovered from their loss, which was the reason they threw themselves deeper into socialising; the less time they were at home, the easier they found it to bear the loss of their beloved daughter.

Charlotte had a deep affection for Emily. "Tell me, George, how is my beautiful niece? Have the newlyweds returned from their honeymoon?"

"They returned two weeks ago, and I have never seen her happier," Lord Leatherby replied, with a look of pride on his face at the mere mention of Emily.

"And you, William, how have you settled back into life at the manor?" she asked, knowing full well that William was quite intolerant of the lifestyle he had been born into. As a child, he could always be found playing with the farmhand's children and hated having to conform to the strict upbringing of the aristocracy, but his family gave him little choice.

Unfortunately for the young master, huge efforts had been made since childhood by the Southwick family and the Leatherbys to push him and Amelia together.

His fate had been sealed, and at the age of nineteen, they became engaged. However, as the engagement was short-lived due to Amelia's pregnancy followed by her suicide, William got the opportunity he had always wanted. He'd left the aristocratic lifestyle behind, much to his father's disapproval, and proceeded to live in a cottage in the Scottish Highlands with only a cook and a maid. For the benefit of the social circle, it had been broadcast that he was recovering from the recent tragic events and was residing with his aristocratic Scottish family.

It had taken three years for William to convince his father that the Leatherby lifestyle wasn't how he wished to spend the rest of his life. He'd agreed to return home provided he was given a productive role to perform at Leatherby and could abandon the whole aristocratic social circle. An agreement was reached, and William accepted the role of estate manager; however, his father insisted that he must attend family events such as Christmas, weddings and funerals—from all non-specific gatherings, he would be excused. William was happy with that arrangement, hence his return to the manor house.

"You know me, Aunt Charlotte, still trying to break with tradition," William replied, displaying a wicked grin, which clearly infuriated his father.

"You're twenty-two now, William. When am I likely to be attending your wedding? Do you have a young lady to speak of?"

Same old Aunt Charlotte, always fishing for information.

"One day no doubt, Aunt Charlotte. I'm sure there is a young lady out there somewhere," he replied very matter-of-factly.

Charlotte was obviously not going to obtain any credible information from her nephew. She rang for Watkins, and arrangements were made to show her guests to their rooms. However, there was still no sign of the two footmen.

"What could possibly be taking them so long?" Lord Leatherby grumbled.

***

Charlie and Arthur were exhausted; they were clearly lost. They'd followed Lord Leatherby's directions to the last detail, or so they thought, but they still appeared to be nowhere near Belgrave Square.

"We should have turned left when I said turn left," Charlie protested.

"But we had already been down that street, twice." By now, Arthur was showing his exasperation.

Their bewildered looks were quickly spotted by a nearby police constable.

"Now, boys, can I be of any help?"

"We need to be here, Officer," Arthur said, showing the constable the directions.

"If you walk straight ahead, turn right, then right again and then take a left, that will bring you to where you need to be."

For the remainder of the walk, they blamed each other for their lack of direction. Eventually, they arrived at their destination just in time to hear the dressing gong as they entered the servants' area.

***

The day of the funeral was a national day of mourning, which meant London saw masses of people arrive to witness the king's state funeral. The gun carriage which bore his coffin travelled from Westminster Hall, where he had been lying in state, through Whitehall, past Hyde Park Corner and Marble Arch until it reached Paddington Station. Taking his place behind the gun carriage and walking in front of important world royalty and dignitaries was the king's dog, a wire fox terrier called Caesar who had been King Edward's inseparable companion. He was led through the streets of London by a kilted highland soldier. There was an impressive horseback procession followed by eleven carriages, all of which took their place behind the king's dog. On arrival at Paddington Station, the funeral train conveyed the coffin and mourners to St George's Chapel at Windsor Castle.

The sombre mood was a complete contrast to the previous day. Edward VII had been well liked, and there were throngs of people lining the streets, all wanting to pay their respects. There was an infinite amount of people but strangely an eerie silence had fallen over London, a feeling of apprehension about what the future would hold under the reign of the new king, George V.

***

Martha had missed Charlie's presence and was thrilled at his return. He was always full of chat and never failed to keep them entertained; the servant's hall was a quieter, less excitable place without him—even Mr Hampton would have openly agreed with that. Having never visited London, Martha was eager to find out as much as she could about the city.

"Well, Charlie, what did London look like? Were there lots of people? Did—"

"One question at a time, Martha," Charlie said, folding his newspaper and making himself comfortable in the armchair by the fire. He leaned forward and, resting his elbows on his knees, he placed his chin in his hands and looked directly at Martha. She dragged one of the hard chairs away from the table and placed it in front of him, anxiously awaiting his reply.

"The first thing we noticed when we left the train station was the streets were paved with gold."

His face remained deadpan waiting for Martha's response.

"No, really! That must have been so pretty."

"Now, lad, don't tease the lass," said Mrs Mead, who had just entered the room. "We all know there are no streets of gold in London."

Martha turned to look at Mrs Mead then turned back to Charlie. She wasn't sure who to believe.

Mrs Mead collected the tea tray then leaned forward and whispered in her ear. "That's the truth, lass. Don't you let him string you a load of old rubbish."

"How many people went to see the king?" Martha asked, hoping that Charlie would continue with his story.

"I couldn't believe my eyes—there were about two million people all lining the streets to watch the coffin go past. They put his coffin on a carriage and all the rich people, the kings and queens from all over the world, followed behind."

Mrs Mead, being a proud royalist, was standing in the doorway, listening intently.

Martha couldn't comprehend that amount of people, not realising that Charlie had greatly exaggerated the crowd figure. It was, in fact, a quarter of a million.

"But the most important of all was the king's dog—he walked right behind the king's coffin and—"

"Charlie Ackworth, you're teasing the lass again. The king's dog indeed," scoffed Mrs Mead.

"Honest, Mrs Mead, that's the truth, honest. Ask Arthur—he saw it too!"

"Well I never. Who'd have thought, the king's dog at the king's funeral." She walked away, shaking her head and tutting to herself.

Martha hadn't moved a muscle. She was absorbing every last bit of information.

"Well, that's it for now. We have work to be getting on with," Charlie said as he collected the newspaper and made his way to the courtyard for a read and a smoke.

Before he could settle himself on the old crate, he was greeted by a young girl about to knock on the door, announcing that she wanted to apply for the housemaid job. The girl followed behind Charlie as he headed towards Mrs Harvey's parlour, hurriedly attempting to keep up with his long strides while at the same time trying to smooth down her windblown hair.

Mrs Harvey was annoyed with herself that she had forgotten to make arrangements for the job vacancy to be removed from Mr Withers' shop window.

"I've walked from the next village. Is the job still here, miss?" the girl asked, her face full of anticipation.

"Actually, there has been a change of plan and we don't need another housemaid at the moment. I—"

"But in the window, it says you do, miss. I saw it, miss."

"Yes, I know. It's my fault, it slipped my mind to make sure that the advert was removed. I am sorry."

The girl looked pitiful, and Mrs Harvey's heart went out to her. She must have walked three miles or more to get here. Her shoes looked as though they were fit for the bin; one of them had a broken strap and was held on with string. The floral summer dress she wore was far too thin for early May. She didn't have a coat or a cardigan, and the dress didn't even have long sleeves. She had an uncontrollable amount of chestnut curls that she kept pushing back off her face. In doing so, she revealed a multitude of freckles, which emphasised her youth. Her eyes looked sad and lacked sparkle despite being the deepest blue, and her tiny face was drawn.

"Will you need one soon, miss?"

Mrs Harvey thought for a moment then said, "What's your name, and how old are you?"

"I'm Dorothy Dawkins. Everybody calls me Dotty, miss, and I'm nearly fifteen, miss."

"Well, Dotty, if you tell me where you live, when we need another housemaid, you will be the first to know." She opened the drawer and handed Dotty a pencil and some paper.

"I don't write, miss. I can tell you though." Dotty averted her eyes and looked embarrassed as she handed the paper and pencil back, but she happily gave Mrs Harvey her address.

"When will I know, miss?"

"I can't tell you for sure, Dotty, but I promise I will let you know."

"Thank you, miss. I best be making my way home now, miss."

Mrs Harvey watched Dotty walk across the courtyard. She turned and waved, shouting, "Bye, miss."

She looked so young and was clearly disappointed.

As soon as I need another housemaid, I will contact you, Dotty. I promise, Mrs Harvey thought as she shut the door and made her way to the kitchen to speak with Mrs Mead.

Chapter 12

Albie had finished work for the day. He stood back and admired his summer bedding display. Happy with the results, he locked his tools in the potting shed and headed home.

His cottage was on the edge of the Leatherby estate. During the summer months, the walk was always pleasant, but the winter months were beginning to take their toll, last winter being particularly harsh. Maybe it was time he thought about retiring.

The walk usually lasted about forty-five minutes; the route through the woods was the quickest. The woodland never failed to trigger memories of his beloved Maud. She'd adored nature and would spend many hours introducing the children from the local school to the wonders of the outdoors. Even after four years, the thought of entering the empty cottage felt like a knife through his heart. He dearly missed her cheerful welcome home and her insistence on discussing the day while enjoying their evening meal.

The cottage was modest but homely. Maud had poured her personality into the décor, and some things remained exactly as they'd been on the day she died. The blue-striped tea towel was still hanging on a hook behind the back door. The scrubbing brush and bucket remained in the yard, and Maud's cardigan had been neatly placed on the back of one of the kitchen chairs. Albie couldn't bring himself to change any of it; somehow, the items were a source of comfort to him.

The uneven path wound through a shady wooded area with a steep grassy bank on one side leading to the river. On both sides of the path, the wild garlic was in full bloom. The smell was pungent and distinctive. The delicate white flowers and long, pointed, oval-shaped leaves coated the woodland floor, displaying their grandeur as far as the eye could see.

Ten minutes into his walk, he heard a noise and halted in his tracks. It sounded like a scream, somebody in distress. He listened hard. There it was again—it was definitely a scream.

"Hello?" he shouted, trying to discern which direction the scream had come from.

Before he had a chance to call a second time, someone barrelled into him, knocking him to the ground. Disoriented, Albie couldn't tell where the man had appeared from, and by the time he managed to pull himself together, the stranger was out of sight. Albie had taken a violent knock, for a man of his advanced years, and was stunned. Before attempting to get up, he shouted again. The voice that responded was that of a young girl.

It sounded as though she could be at the bottom of the steep bank. He slowly pulled himself up and struggled to peer over the edge.

He was right—the injured party was a young girl. She appeared to have tumbled the length of the bank and landed in a heap at the bottom. There was a look of urgency on her little face.

"It's my ankle! I needs help, mister," the girl shouted.

Albie was unable to comprehend how he could safely descend the slippery bank, let alone climb back up while trying to help the injured girl. He needed help.

Reassuring her that he would return, he made every effort to hurry, but moving at pace had long since passed Albie by.

"Mr Hampton! Mr Hampton!" he shouted as he approached the end of the woodland path. He was seriously out of breath.

"Albie, are you all right? What's happened?"

Mr Hampton was returning from the village. It was still deemed unsafe for the housemaids to leave the estate alone, so Mr Hampton had been running errands more and more recently.

"Goodness, you can hardly breathe. Sit, sit down," he insisted.

Albie flopped to the ground. It was a relief to be sitting down. By now, he was gasping for breath, coughing and spluttering, unable to provide Mr Hampton with any information. Eventually, he caught his breath and the coughing subsided. He attempted to stand up but lost his balance slightly, so promptly sat down again.

"Stay seated, man," Mr Hampton ordered him abruptly. "Now, tell me slowly what the problem is."

Albie wouldn't remain seated; he was determined to stand, and the second attempt was a little easier. He provided Mr Hampton with a detailed account of what had happened, stopping periodically to cough and catch his breath.

The two men realised they were going to require some young blood to perform the rescue operation.

Albie waited while Mr Hampton went to the house. By the time the butler returned, he was red-faced and breathing heavily, accompanied by a worried-looking Ed.

Eventually, the young girl was rescued. Her ankle was badly swollen, and she was unable to put any weight on it; her calf was also bleeding. Ed tied a handkerchief he found lying on the floor alongside her tightly around her injured leg. Then, picking her up with ease and taking gigantic strides, he climbed the steep bank effortlessly while Mr Hampton and Albie looked on.

Ed carried the young girl to Mrs Harvey's parlour. He placed her in the comfort of the housekeeper's chair and waited with her until Mrs Harvey arrived.

"Good grief, what on earth happened to you two?" was Mrs Mead's response when she entered the kitchen and saw Albie and Mr Hampton, dishevelled and in an obvious state of weariness.

Mr Hampton's perfectly oiled hair was ruffled and the front of it was randomly flopping across his forehead. He was still red in the face, and his butler attire was worse for wear. He was leaning on the table with his head in his hands, shaking it back and forth.

Albie was having trouble catching his breath and was coughing profusely.

"Here, drink this, for goodness' sake. You'll wake the graveyard if you keep that up," Mrs Mead said, handing him a large glass of water.

***

When Mrs Harvey entered her parlour, she was aghast to see Dotty clearly in distress and injured.

"Dotty," she said, crossing the room to comfort her.

She placed her arms around the young girl and pulled her close.

"I didn't see him, miss," Dotty said, unable to control her sobs. "He grabbed me, miss, but then he fell and I did too, and I landed at the bottom of the bank by the river, miss."

"Who, Dotty? Who grabbed you?"

"Don't know, miss. Didn't see him much. Then the old man saw me and got help. He helped me," Dotty said, pointing at Ed, "and the man in the black suit—he helped as well."

"Ed, could you ask Mrs Mead for a bowl of hot water, some bandages and a strap for this ankle? And a glass of water as well, please."

Ed left the room, immediately passing Mr Hampton en route. Before knocking, the butler tried in vain to remove some of the mud from his normally pristine uniform.

"Come in," Mrs Harvey shouted.

Mr Hampton entered, still looking slightly red in the face, but he had made an attempt to control his loose locks.

"How is this young lady feeling now?" he asked, looking at Dotty with a deep worry in his eyes.

Then it dawned on Mrs Harvey that the man in the black suit had been Mr Hampton.

While Dotty's leg wound was being cleaned and her ankle strapped, Mr Hampton questioned her gently but learned nothing more about her attacker.

Mrs Harvey removed the handkerchief from Dotty's leg. She placed it to one side and proceeded to bandage the wound and then strap her ankle.

"Dotty, can you tell me where you found this handkerchief?" she said, giving Mr Hampton a look of concern.

"I didn't find it, miss. It was on the floor by where I fell and the lad picked it up to tie on my leg, miss."

Mr Hampton picked the handkerchief up to examine it closer. Even with the bloodstains from Dotty's wound, the initials embroidered in one of the corners were still visible, as clear as day.

It was obvious that Dotty couldn't walk home that day or possibly for the next few. Ed carried her upstairs and placed her on the bed in Rosie's old room. Mrs Harvey followed with a nightgown, a jug of water and some fresh towels. Dotty was physically drained, so she didn't protest when Mrs Harvey tucked her into bed.

"My mam will be worried, miss," Dotty said, trying her very best to stay awake.

"Don't you worry about that; one of the stable lads will run an errand with a note to reassure your family that you are safe. Mrs Mead will send Elsie along in a little while with a tray. And now you must try to get some rest."

"I will, miss."

By the time Mrs Harvey had gathered the small bundle of sorrowful-looking clothes for the laundry, Dotty was asleep. Mrs Harvey studied her closely; she looked so very young. Dotty Dawson, she thought, I don't think you are almost fifteen.

After disposing of Dotty's clothes in the laundry room, Mrs Harvey knew she must speak to Mr Hampton as a matter of urgency. The initials on the white handkerchief could possibly bear the identity of the attacker. Constable Jennings would need to be informed of yet another attack, and His Lordship had to be told.

She found Mr Hampton in his office with a glass of sherry, and another he'd poured for her. The blood-stained handkerchief was carefully placed on a chair.

"Well, have you any idea who it could possibly belong to?" she asked, immediately accepting the glass of sherry.

"No, absolutely no idea, Mrs Harvey. Do you think the three attacks are linked to the same person?"

"Yes, I do, Mr Hampton. I am sure of it," she replied, nodding her head. She bent forward to take a more detailed look at the handkerchief.

The next step was to speak to Lord Leatherby and contact Constable Jennings. It was late evening, and the family had already retired to the drawing room following dinner.

While Mr Hampton went to fetch His Lordship, Mrs Harvey waited for them both in the library, pacing back and forth as she turned the situation over in her mind. Eventually, Lord Leatherby, wearing an irritated scowl, burst through the door.

"What on earth is going on, Hampton, Mrs Harvey?"

Mr Hampton reiterated the events that had led to finding the white handkerchief. He explained that Dotty was unable to walk home and was asleep in one of the servant bedrooms. Mrs Harvey produced the handkerchief, making certain the initials were clearly visible to His Lordship. The instant he saw them, his pallor changed dramatically. He took the handkerchief off Mrs Harvey and examined it closer. There was no mistake.

"Leave this with me. I'll contact Jennings. Thank you, that will be all."

***

With the servants gone, Lord Leatherby poured himself a drink and walked towards the fireplace. Staring into the flames, he crumpled the handkerchief into a ball, but then, he faltered. Destroying the evidence was not the answer. He gulped his drink then poured another. His mind was racing. If he withheld evidence from Jennings, he would be committing a criminal offence, and if he didn't, life at Leatherby Manor would never be quite the same again.

Hesitantly, he rang for Mr Hampton.

"Hampton, contact Jennings. Advise him there has been a development with regard to the investigation, and I would appreciate him calling tonight."

He returned to the drawing room, where little had changed since he left thirty minutes earlier. His wife was still seated facing the fireplace, radiant in a deep purple full-length cocktail dress and long black velvet gloves. She was wearing the gold choker with an amethyst teardrop that had been his gift to celebrate their twentieth wedding anniversary. The heat from the fire had given a glow to her cheeks. He thought how much younger she looked than her forty-two years.

William was leaning against the imposing inglenook fire surround, resting his arm on the mantel and clutching a whiskey glass in the other hand. Lord Leatherby remembered how ecstatic his wife had been when William's letter arrived, confirming he was returning after what she had described as three long years. At last, William seemed to feel he had a purpose in life and had thrown himself wholeheartedly into the position of estate manager; he was content, and it pleased his mother.

Deep in conversation, seated side by side on the plush green sofa, were Emily and her new husband, who she adored. They were oblivious to any other person in the room, which was exactly how it should be. They were, after all, newlyweds and still in the first flush of marital bliss.

Mr Hampton introduced Constable Jennings into the drawing room, much to the curiosity of everyone. Lord Leatherby crossed the room to stand directly in front of the fireplace and address his family.

"I have requested the company of Constable Jennings as there has been a development in the investigations concerning the recent attacks. Today there was another attack, which now totals three. However, this time there was evidence left at the scene."

An unnerving silence descended on the room. All eyes were fixed on Lord Leatherby. They looked on in bewilderment as he removed the white, bloodstained handkerchief from his pocket and explained that it was the evidence he had referred to earlier. The initials at this point were not on display; he had purposely not exposed them. He walked to Constable Jennings and handed him the handkerchief. The constable unfolded it fully. The initials H A E were clearly visible.

"I believe this belongs to you?" Lord Leatherby said, directing his question to Henry Albert Enson, Lady Emily's husband.

Instantly, Henry broke down, head in his hands, sobbing like a baby. He started to repeat over and over again that he was sorry. Turning to Emily, he looked directly into her eyes, emphasising his remorse.

Her colour had drained. She looked ashen-faced but remained composed. Ignoring his pathetic pleas, she stood up and left the drawing room, tears beginning to fall. Her mother hastily stood up and called after her.

"Emily, darling, wait!"

"No, Mother. No," was Emily's brusque reply.

Lady Leatherby sat back down, respecting the fact that her daughter wanted to be alone.

William didn't utter a word. He strolled toward the window, stood for a while, then very calmly turned and looked directly at Henry. "Well, are you responsible for all three attacks?"

Henry's eyes were firmly fixed on the floor, both hands across the back of his neck. He was still sobbing pathetically. He didn't reply; he just nodded.

Constable Jennings had been scribbling all the details into his notebook. Mr Hampton looked on in shock and anger. He must have seen the initials but not recognised them, Lord Leatherby realised. The staff only ever addressed Henry as Master Enson.

"So, you say you were responsible for all three attacks," Constable Jennings said. "In that case, you would have received a blow to the head from the first incident." Jennings quickly checked his notes. "Struck by a vase, I believe?"

Henry slowly removed his hands from the back of his neck and pushed aside a small section of hair to display a well-healed scar near his temple. Lady Leatherby had seen and heard enough. She stood up abruptly and, displaying utter disgust towards her son-in-law, she bid everybody a good night and all but marched out of the room.

"There's something else," Henry announced.

The sobbing had abruptly stopped, and he appeared unruffled. He turned to face William. In a callous tone, he confessed to being the father of Lady Amelia's baby.

Henry Enson had loathed William from a young age. William was the more handsome of the two men, the more intelligent and infinitely the more popular within the aristocratic circle. Henry had adored Amelia and was distraught when her engagement was announced. When he'd declared his love for her, he was bitterly angry at how little interest she showed towards him. He couldn't accept this and, in desperation, attempted to persuade her otherwise. The situation became out of hand, and he forced himself upon her. When she'd realised she was pregnant, she couldn't carry the disgrace. Just like Rosie, she'd refused to divulge the truth. The two young women were worlds apart; they had nothing in common besides finding themselves in the same heartbreaking situation. They'd felt the same shame, the same pain and hopelessness and shed the same tears for a plight they knew could have only one ending.

William had been suspected of Amelia's death. He'd lived through hell until the inquest declared suicide. Henry had almost ruined William—but he didn't stop there. His next plan was to woo Emily, knowing that if he married into the family, he would be in a position to continue his reign of malice against William. He was well aware that Lord Leatherby hated the fact that his only son had opted out of the aristocratic lifestyle. As the lord's son, he should have been duty-bound to fulfil the role of heir. Henry's plan had been to manipulate the situation between father and son with the goal of taking William's inheritance. However, he had developed an appetite for his sordid and lustful behaviour. He had become complacent, and this had eventually led to his downfall.

William flew across the room, temper seething, and knocked Henry roughly to the floor. Lord Leatherby and Jennings intervened, separating the two men. Henry was no longer a snivelling wreck; he was cold and heartless, showing no remorse. Lord Leatherby looked at him with disgust. The thought that this man had married his daughter and had been living under his roof revolted him.

Both he and William were relieved when Constable Jennings made the arrest and led the insensitive and calculating Henry Enson away.

***

Mrs Harvey was anxiously waiting to speak to Mr Hampton. After the meeting in the library, she had returned to her room to await the outcome. The servants were aware of the attack on Dotty but had no knowledge of the handkerchief, and she intended to keep it that way until the matter had been resolved.

Eventually, there was a knock on her door.

"Come in," she shouted.

When Mr Hampton entered, he looked dazed. The sadness in his eyes seemed to age him instantly.

"Sit down before you fall down. You look dreadful," Mrs Harvey said, moving her armchair forward.

She handed him a small glass of sherry and made herself comfortable on one of the hard-back chairs, then reached for the decanter and poured herself a drink. Respectfully, she didn't question him. She waited until he felt ready to divulge what had occurred when Constable Jennings had arrived.

Slowly and deliberately, Mr Hampton conveyed the distressing scene that had taken place in the drawing room. He detailed the ugliness of it, and as he did, his hands began to shake. It had obviously affected him dreadfully.

Mrs Harvey listened without making any interruptions. Mr Hampton's words churned her stomach. Her fingers tightened around the sherry glass, and she poured herself another drink quickly.

"Oh, Mr Hampton, it's all my fault Rosie is dead and Dotty was attacked," she said, raising her hand to her mouth and shaking her head.

"How could that possibly be? The fault is with that monster I witnessed earlier."

"If I hadn't insisted that Rosie make the journey to the village with the notice for a new housemaid, she would still be alive. The poor girl didn't want to go; she told me the weather was going to become worse, but I insisted. I made her go, Mr Hampton, and now she's dead. And

Dotty, poor Dotty. If I had remembered to remove the advert from the shop window, little Dotty wouldn't have seen it, and then…" She couldn't continue. She put both hands up to her face and cried bitterly, consumed with guilt.

Mr Hampton stood up to comfort her. He gently lowered both hands from her face and squeezed them affectionately, doing his utmost to reassure her.

"Now, now, you have no need to be upsetting yourself. Not you or anybody else could have imagined the attacks."

***

The events of the night had impacted upstairs enormously, just as Lord Leatherby had predicted. Emily had vacated the drawing room bravely; however, once in the privacy of her own room, she'd crumbled. The enormity of what her husband had confessed to was unthinkable. She glanced around the bedroom and felt repulsed at the sight of his belongings, haphazardly displayed. The anger in her swelled, and she lashed out, throwing anything associated with Henry to the floor. The noise sent her father and William racing upstairs. William took firm hold of Emily's shoulders, compelling her to stop the destruction. She gave in and collapsed heavily against his chest. Lord and Lady Leatherby looked on in despair as their son gathered Emily into his arms and placed her into bed like a baby. He sat with her until she finally fell into a fretful sleep.

Chapter 13

The following morning, Mrs Harvey woke with a heavy heart. She couldn't shake the feeling of guilt that was weighing her down. Her thoughts kept returning to what Rosie must have endured and how frightened she must have been. But Dotty was her priority now, and she was eager to check on her. She asked Elsie to prepare a breakfast tray and took it up to the girl herself.

"Dotty, it's Mrs Harvey. Are you awake?" she called as she opened the door.

She was relieved to see Dotty sitting up in bed, looking brighter and calmer than she had the day before.

"Morning, miss. Is that for me?" she asked, eyes widening at the sight of the breakfast tray.

"Yes, you must be hungry—although I can see you've eaten the food Elsie left for you."

"Yes, miss, I woke up and was so hungry I ate it all, miss," Dotty said, sounding apologetic.

Mrs Harvey left Dotty to enjoy her breakfast. As she was about to leave the room, Dotty asked, "Miss, did my mam get a note about me?"

"Yes, Dotty, your mother knows that you are safe. The stable lad delivered the note. Now eat up, and I'll be back later."

***

By the time Mrs Harvey had returned downstairs, Master William was waiting for her. He had taken control of the unfortunate situation that the upstairs household had found themselves in. The first item on his list was to speak with Martha.

The servants were aware something untoward had taken place, especially as Ethel was moping around and feeling sorry for herself. She had been told that she would not be required to assist Lady Emily until further notice, and as a result, had been assigned to housemaid duties. "Didn't see that coming, did she?" Charlie said in his most sarcastic tone, about to help himself to his second cup of tea and settle down to read the newspaper.

Before he addressed the rest of the servants, William wanted to tell Martha personally who her attacker had been and to prepare her for the possibility that she may be called as a witness in the trial. When Martha entered the room, he had an overwhelming desire to scoop her into his arms. He hated the thought of what she had suffered at the hands of Henry and wished she had confided in him on the journey back to the manor house. But he knew protocol would have prevailed, enforced by Mrs Harvey and Mr Hampton. Martha had abided by the rules, making Mrs Harvey her first point of contact in any situation. Upstairs would always be informed secondarily.

William took her to one side to speak to her. She listened and nodded, grateful, but he could see her sorrow when he told her of Emily's plight, and she appeared noticeably unnerved at the thought of the trial. He wished he could have taken more time to console her, but she was soon snatched away by her duties.

Next on William's list was to address the rest of the staff. They gathered in the servants' hall, awaiting his arrival.

Everybody snapped to attention and stood up as William entered the room. He gestured for them to sit down and started his address. There was not a sound made; you could have heard a pin drop. It was difficult for them to make sense of what he was saying. Only weeks previous, they had been preparing for the most extravagant wedding, and now this. Master William finished what he intended to say, bid them good morning and left.

"Well, would you believe it? Master Enson. Who would have thought…"

"Yes, yes, that is more than enough, Mrs Mead. Everybody on with your work," Mrs Harvey said as she waved her arms for them to leave the room.

***

Dotty appeared to be recovering well from her ordeal. She was hobbling around the bedroom when Mrs Harvey returned with her clothes. When she was dressed, Ed carried her downstairs, placing her once again in the armchair in Mrs Harvey's room.

"There you go, lass. I'm glad to see you look so much better today," he said and left the room as Mrs Harvey appeared.

The first question she wanted to ask Dotty was about her age.

"Dotty, are you really almost fifteen?"

Dotty didn't answer straight away. She sighed heavily and, shrugging her shoulders, said, "No, miss. Nearly thirteen, miss. I thought I would get the job if I said I was older, miss. We needs the money in the house, miss, my dad don't work no more and…"

Mrs Harvey stopped her. "It's all right, Dotty, I understand."

Without warning, Dotty began to cry. There was something about this little ragamuffin girl that was pulling at Mrs Harvey's heartstrings.

"I won't be long, Dotty," she said, and she left the room to speak with Mr Hampton and Mrs Mead.

"What is it, Mrs Harvey? What's so important?" Mrs Mead asked, her attention clearly elsewhere. As usual, the kitchen was hectic and both she and Elsie were run off their feet.

Mr Hampton entered the kitchen, but before either of them could speak, Mrs Harvey asked, "Mr Hampton, Mrs Mead, would you object if I offered Dotty a position of scullery maid? Elsie could more than do with the help."

Mrs Mead was unsure and didn't mince her words. "She's very young, Mrs Harvey. She would be of no help to me if she was to get under my feet."

Mr Hampton said he couldn't see a problem with the request and left the two women to work it out between themselves.

Eventually, the housekeeper and the cook agreed. Mrs Harvey was thrilled and clasped her hands together in anticipation of giving Dotty the good news.

Dotty was overjoyed at being offered a job.

"Scullery maid, miss? Me, miss? Thank you, thank you, miss."

"Just one thing, Dotty. Could you stop calling me miss? Mrs Harvey will do nicely."

"Yes, I will, I will, miss."

***

After performing housemaid's duties for a number of weeks, Ethel was ecstatic to make an announcement to her fellow servants.

"Everybody, attention, please! I'm going to live in London," she broadcast loud and clear as she made her entrance into the servants' hall.

Charlie laughed out loud. "In your dreams, Ethel Brooks."

"Well, it must be a good dream, Charlie Ackworth, because I'm going tomorrow," she said triumphantly, and then, turning sharply on her heels, she left the room.

There was a shocked silence from her audience.

"Well, would you believe it? Little Miss Nosey Parker off to London to see the streets paved with gold," Charlie said, as he threw Martha a wink.

***

Lady Emily had rarely left her room in the three weeks since the fateful night. She'd informed William that she wanted all links with Henry out of her life, and that included Leatherby Manor. William had exhausted every avenue of encouragement and cajoling, but her mind was made up. She wrote to Charlotte in London, requesting to live with her and Edward in Belgrave Square. Her intention was to take only a few personal belongings and Ethel. Everything else was tainted. She'd have to purchase a completely new wardrobe. All her dresses, shoes, coats, hats and bags held a memory of a time spent with Henry.

Charlotte was more than happy to accommodate her niece; she loved her dearly and would relish spending time with her. She arrived at Leatherby Manor, considering herself to be Emily's saving grace. Although her intention was to stay for only one night, her luggage suggested otherwise. The minute she set eyes on her brother, she was aghast at the amount of weight he had lost and the gauntness of his face.

"My goodness, George, have you not eaten since that dreadful man was arrested? You look ghastly," she said as she made her way to the drawing room.

"It's nice to see you too, Charlotte. As you can imagine, life has been difficult, but we are confident that a few weeks spent with you in London will help Emily enormously," he said, the optimism straining his voice.

Charlotte had never been known for her tact. Though she knew it wasn't what her brother wanted to hear, she was going to say it anyway.

"George, you mustn't be under any illusion: this is going to take far more than a few weeks, and you must be prepared for Emily to remain in London for some considerable time."

Her brother's shoulders lowered, and his face looked full of despair. She could tell he just wanted his heartbroken daughter to be well, for everything to be back to normal. But after all this, Emily couldn't stay here. She needed to distance herself from all the hurtful memories.

So, with a deep sorrow in his eyes, Lord Leatherby gave her up to Charlotte and London.

***

That evening, Ethel was unbearable. Her continual chatter irritated Charlie.

"I, for one, will be glad when she is on the train to London—hopefully with a one-way ticket," he whispered to Martha, who found it difficult to control a fit of giggles.

Muriel was suffering from a serious attack of jealousy. As the longer-serving lady's maid, she felt it should be her travelling to London with Lady Emily, despite the fact she was lady's maid to Her Ladyship. The atmosphere and bickering didn't go unnoticed; Muriel and Ethel were summoned to Mrs Harvey's parlour, and thankfully, peace between them had been restored by the time they returned.

The following morning, Charlotte and Lady Emily, with Ethel in tow, left to take the early London train. William and his parents waved Emily goodbye at the station, not knowing when she would feel strong enough to return to Leatherby Manor. It was a sad day, and it weighed heavy on Lord Leatherby's mind. He adored his daughter, and suddenly she felt lost to him. He had no indication as to when they would enjoy each other's company again without the sour taste of Henry Enson and what he had been capable of.

The impact of Enson's actions had also greatly affected downstairs. Martha was concerned about the impending trial, and not a day passed without her fretting about it. It wasn't certain she would be required to attend, but it was a possibility, and that worried her.

Mrs Harvey had taken Dotty under her wing. It was her way of trying to make amends. She still blamed herself for the attack on Dotty and the rape that had led to Rosie's suicide. It pleased her to see that Dotty's injuries had healed and she had settled in well to life downstairs.

As a scullery maid, Dotty was below Elsie in the servant ranks. This boosted Elsie's self-esteem, as she was in a position now to assert her authority as a kitchen maid, where Dotty was concerned. The scullery maid's duties were to clean and peel the vegetables; wash dishes and rub the saucepans, kettles and pots; and light the kitchen fires in the morning, all of which Elsie had been performing on top of her kitchen duties. Now with Dotty in the role of scullery maid, Elsie had the time to take more care with the cooking duties assigned to her by Mrs Mead. Dotty's help was invaluable; she worked diligently from the instant she woke until her last duty was complete at the end of the day. However, there was no endorsement from Mrs Mead regarding Dotty's work ethic. It would be some time before she would receive such praise, a long time indeed.

Chapter 14

It was unusual for Mr Hampton to interrupt luncheon, and William knew something serious must have happened the moment he saw the butler's grave expression.

"Sorry to disturb you, my lord. Constable Jennings wishes to speak with you."

"Well, show him in, Hampton."

"He is waiting on the telephone line, my lord, in the hall."

William and Lady Leatherby waited in anticipation as Lord Leatherby took the call. He promptly returned to the dining room.

He leaned forward in his chair, placed his elbows on the table and clasped his hands together. He then announced, very calmly, "This family will not be required to suffer a trial. Enson hung himself last night."

Lady Leatherby gasped aloud. William could only imagine the relief she must have felt—the idea of a trial had been worrying his mother to the point where she had been feeling quite unwell.

William stood up immediately.

"Would you excuse me? There is a matter I need to attend to," he said as he hurriedly left the dining room and ran down to the housekeeper's parlour.

"Mrs Harvey, where's Martha?" he asked, sounding slightly out of breath.

"It's her birthday. She's taken advantage of the time off she's allowed and is paying a visit to Rosie's grave, sir. She left about half an hour since."

William thanked Mrs Harvey and headed across the courtyard to the potting shed, where he was hoping to find Albie.

"Albie, I need some flowers—any flowers. No—roses. I need roses." William's tone was urgent.

"What colour would you like, sir? There are pink and there are—"

"Any colour, Albie, but I need them quickly. Can you do that for me?"

"Well, yes, sir, I can. Follow me to the rose garden."

Albie eventually handed William a bouquet of delicate pink, white and pale lavender roses, from which he had painstakingly removed every thorn.

"You're the second person today, sir, to ask for flowers. Martha the housemaid wanted some of my chrysanthemums to take to that poor girl's grave."

William was grateful to Albie for being so helpful, but he wished the old man had worked a little faster. He was longing to speak with Martha.

The village church was a twenty-minute walk from the manor. As he entered the churchyard, he saw Martha. She was kneeling beside the grave, poignantly talking to her friend. He was struck, as he always was, by her loveliness. He had never seen her vibrant auburn hair loose, but today it flowed across her shoulders, displaying a golden shimmer from the afternoon sun. As she stood up, he noted how petite she was, her small frame more obvious in the thin cotton summer dress.

As she turned to leave the churchyard, she was startled to see him standing there.

"Hello, Martha. I have some good news for you," he said, walking towards her. "You won't be required to attend the trial."

"Oh, sir, that is good news; I have been so worried, sir. Can you tell me why, sir?" she asked.

"Last night, Henry Enson hung himself. Constable Jennings gave us the news during luncheon."

Martha didn't appear shocked; she broke into a beaming smile, and her eyes danced with happiness and relief. Then, she gestured at the roses and said, "Don't forget to put them on Rosie's grave, sir. Beautiful roses for beautiful Rosie." She smiled, melting William's heart in the process.

"They are for you, Martha," he said. "Happy birthday."

"But sir, how—"

"Mrs Harvey told me it was your birthday and where I could find you."

"Thank you, sir." Martha took the roses off him, her head slightly bowed, displaying a sweet shyness.

They were comfortable in each other's company, enjoying the walk back to the house and falling easily into conversation. Martha spoke mainly about her family and how much she missed them, especially on days like today. She told him that birthdays were always happy times in her house. Her mother would make a special birthday tea and never failed to bake a cake.

"When was the last time you saw your family, Martha?" he asked.

"Christmas, sir," she said, and sighed heavily.

He thought for a moment, then stopped abruptly, turned to look at her and said, "You will see them today—yes, today. On your birthday. When we arrive at the house, I'll collect the car and drive you home to see your family."

Martha stopped in her tracks, her eyes wide. She was completely taken aback by William's suggestion.

"But sir, I have duties this evening, my time off will finish soon, and Mrs Harvey will—"

"Don't you worry about Mrs Harvey. Leave her to me."

He caught hold of her hand, and they ran the last part of their journey, hand in hand.

William rushed into the servants' quarter and in his haste almost knocked Mrs Harvey to the floor in the narrow corridor.

"Sorry, so sorry. You have to excuse Martha from duties this evening," he said, talking at such speed Mrs Harvey struggled to follow.

Martha was standing alongside William, proudly holding her bouquet of roses. However, now face to face with Mrs Harvey, the uneasiness in her stance looked as if she were about to bolt.

Turning to Martha, Mrs Harvey asked, "Are you not well?"

Before she had a chance to reply, William leapt in to answer. "Martha is very well, Mrs Harvey. I'm going to drive her to see her family, and we will be leaving right away. Could you ask Hampton to arrange for the car to be driven around to the courtyard entrance? Thank you, Mrs Harvey."

They turned around and were about to head out of the servants' area towards the entrance of the courtyard when Mrs Harvey called after Martha. "Would you like me to put those flowers in water?"

"Oh, yes, Mrs Harvey, thank you," she said, handing her the roses.

Martha was bubbling with excitement when she caught up with William and they headed out to the car. He had spotted the two footmen as he'd walked through the corridor—they had obviously been eavesdropping. He had no doubt gossip would follow. Mr Hampton would be sure to have a sour face. Presumably, he thought this to be a step too far, even for the rebellious young master, but William didn't care.

William knew that when he returned his father would be waiting for him armed with a lecture. He had reluctantly accepted William's dislike of the lifestyle he had been born into, but when he was informed of the day's events, he would be consumed with anger. William was not concerned. He felt carefree, enjoying every minute of Martha's company. This was the happiest he had felt for as long as he could remember.

***

Martha felt strangely comfortable and relaxed seated next to William and was ready to embrace the journey. The scenery was spectacular. It was the middle of June, and the trees were laden with their summer foliage. Fields had turned red with a glorious display of poppies. Scattered between the scarlet blooms were beautifully delicate blue cornflowers and a multitude of glorious long-stem moon daisies, each proudly displaying a vivid yellow centre and starch-white petals.

An hour later, the little row of miners' cottages was in sight. Martha started to feel nervous at the thought of introducing Master William to her family. Then suddenly she had an awful thought and asked William what the time was. She was relieved when he confirmed it was 5:15. Her father and brother would have definitely finished using the tin bath. They would be well presented in their newly washed and ironed clothes.

As the car drove slowly along the street where Martha had grown up, she watched some of the children playing leapfrog. A group of little girls were skipping, and there were two young lads sword fighting with sticks. The children were dumbstruck at the sight of the car, abandoning their play instantly. When the car stopped, the boys who had been sword fighting were the first children to approach the vehicle. They stood as close as they dared and stretched on tiptoe to look into the car. The girls didn't approach as closely; they huddled together and looked on from a distance.

"Hey, mister! I'm gonna have a car like that when I grow up," one of the sword fighters shouted.

"Well, good for you!" William called back.

"It's this cottage here, sir," Martha said, walking towards the open front door.

They stepped into the tiny entrance, and Martha pushed open the door to the front room. William followed closely behind.

"Hello, everyone," Martha said, standing in the doorway, shadowed by William. "Mam, Dad, this is Master

William from the manor house." Her voice was slightly shaky.

"Oh my love, it's so nice to see you, and on your birthday as well. Happy birthday, love, happy birthday," Martha's mother said, flinging her arms around her daughter and delivering an enormous hug.

"Well, come in—don't be standing in the doorway. Come in, come in," Martha's dad said as he stood up from the table to shake William's hand. "Nice to meet you, lad."

"Dad, it's sir—you got to call Master William, sir," Martha said, embarrassed.

"No, no, please. My name is William. Please, call me William."

After the initial greetings, there wasn't a trace of tension as the family welcomed William in. Martha was thrilled to see her brother Tommy again, and Tilly was following her around, hanging on her every word for stories about the big house. Martha's mam was the perfect hostess and without any hesitation, she laid a further two places. She proceeded to make the meal stretch to enough food for everyone. All too soon, Martha and William had to leave, but not before they all sang Happy Birthday and a freshly baked birthday cake appeared. Even though Martha wasn't meant to be there on her birthday, a cake had still been baked. After lots of hugs and kisses, eventually, they left the little cottage and set off on their journey back to Leatherby Manor.

"Thank you, sir. I've had such a lovely birthday," Martha said, turning to face William.

"That was the idea. I'm pleased you enjoyed it. But just one thing—I would like you to call me William."

"I will try, William," she said, which made them both laugh.

It was dark by the time they reached the house, and Martha suddenly felt nervous about the reaction she would receive when she entered the servants' hall. William stopped the car at the entrance to the courtyard.

Turning to Martha, he said, "I've had a wonderful day, and your family were so welcoming. We will visit again."

"Thank you so much, sir—I mean William. I would like that very much. I better go in now, good night."

Then she got out of the car and walked away into the darkness of the courtyard.

It was a hot summer evening, the door to the servants' area was wide open, and Charlie and Nell were sitting on the steps.

"The wanderer returns," Charlie shouted as he saw Martha approaching.

Martha was grateful it was dark, as she could feel her cheeks flushing at Charlie's remark.

"Did you have a wonderful time?" Nell asked eagerly.

"Oh, I did, Nell, I really did. But I'm sorry I left you on your own," Martha said as she tried to squeeze past Charlie.

"She's worked her fingers to the bone, she has, while you been off with the master," Charlie piped up in between puffing on his cigarette.

Nell elbowed him in the ribs and said, "Don't listen to him, Martha. Little Dotty helped me, and she was as good as gold, she was."

Martha walked towards Mrs Harvey's room. The door was open, and she could hear Mr Hampton's voice.

"Yes, he was furious. Master William is in for a right dressing down when he returns. And as if His Lordship hasn't got enough to worry about with Lady Emily."

Martha stopped; she didn't have the courage to enter the room and face them both after what she had just heard. Shame welled up inside her at the realisation she was responsible for causing His Lordship more upset. This weighed heavy on her mind.

As she climbed the stairs, she became downcast and full of guilt. In her room, William's roses had been placed in the little vase Rosie had bought her for Christmas. Somebody had carefully trimmed the stems and arranged them beautifully. As sad as she now felt, they brought a smile to her face, especially as they reminded her of William.

Chapter 15

"Did you have a good day, sir?" enquired the chauffeur as William left the car in his capable hands.

"Yes, very good, thank you, Denton. Goodnight."

"Good night, sir."

William had no intention of facing his father's wrath this late in the evening. He strode past the manor and took the path that led to the lake at the bottom of the estate. The light breeze cut smoothly through the sultry night air, and the full moon cast a silvery beam across the blackness of the lake. William sat at the water's edge, calmed by the sound of the soothing ripples, courtesy of the multitude of fish inhabiting the lake. The perfect setting—or it would be, if Martha was at his side.

He was aware that the following day would bring a confrontation with his father. His mother would be easier to deal with—she wanted what William wanted and had accepted that her son's path through life would not be a carbon copy of his father's. Nevertheless, he still had a challenging road ahead of him. Even his mother might find it difficult to accept his intention to include Martha in the rest of his life.

***

Martha slept very little that night. She had loved every minute of her day with William, but it had been overshadowed by the conversation she had heard between Mrs Harvey and Mr Hampton. The fact that her attic room was stifling, and the window would only open a fraction didn't help.

She left her room far earlier than she needed to and sat in the courtyard, listening to the early morning birdsong. She followed the cotton-wool clouds as they glided across the sky, which was still displaying a combination of delicate pink and shimmering gold as a result of a spectacular sunrise. Her thoughts turned to William, but she quickly pushed them out of her mind. She knew there was going to be trouble, and she was the cause of it.

Eventually, there was no more delaying it. She went back inside.

"Morning, Dotty. Thank you for helping yesterday, it was kind of you," Martha said as she collected her housemaid's box and prepared Nell's cleaning supplies.

"I liked it, I did," Dotty replied. "I saw lots of posh things upstairs I never saw before, and I put your flowers in the vase."

Martha thanked her again, leaving her to continue with her work. She didn't want Mrs Mead shouting at the poor girl if the fire wasn't ready.

***

Mrs Harvey poured herself a second cup of tea, hoping it would help to prepare her for the day ahead. Firstly, she needed to speak with Martha, and then she would require a large amount of tolerance to cope with Mr Hampton's bad mood due to the impending fallout from upstairs.

Martha entered Mrs Harvey's room looking sheepish, and before Mrs Harvey had uttered a word, Martha was full of apologies.

"I'm sorry, I shouldn't have gone, but William—I mean the master—he asked me and I wanted to see my family so much and then—"

"That's enough, Martha. Nobody is blaming you. I just need you to realise that this sort of thing won't go anywhere, so don't you have any ideas. It was only the master showing his thoughtful side. He just felt sorry for you; that's all and nothing else. Do you understand, Martha?"

Martha flinched against the stern words and harsh tone.

"Yes, I do understand, Mrs Harvey," she said, sounding timid and very close to tears.

***

William braced himself for the onslaught he was about to receive at breakfast. As he entered the dining room, the stony atmosphere was apparent immediately. This was going to be between William and his father; Lady Leatherby was taking breakfast in her room.

William couldn't face any food from the perfectly laid out breakfast buffet. He took his seat at the dining table and signalled for Charlie to serve the coffee. At that point, Lord Leatherby meticulously folded his newspaper and laid it to the side of him on the table.

In a calm and controlled manner, he looked directly at William and said, "Your reasons for yesterday's little escapade are what, may I ask?"

Before William replied to his father, he dismissed Charlie.

"I have just one reason, and that was to spend time with Martha," was William's casual reply.

His father's face was stern, and the muscle in his jaw flinched several times.

"This cannot and will not happen again, do you understand?" he said, as he thumped the table with his fist and stood up, glaring at his son.

William was unperturbed by his father's outburst. He had witnessed similar on many occasions.

"As my lifestyle will not be following the Leatherby route, there is no reason why I should not pursue my feelings for Martha."

"Have you lost your senses? She is just a housemaid."

"I am well aware of that, and I am just an estate manager who will be living in a cottage on the estate. Therefore, I fail to see the problem."

In his temper, Lord Leatherby snatched the newspaper and stormed out of the dining room. William remained, finished his coffee, then left to begin his work on the estate.

That evening at dinner, Lord Leatherby announced that Charlotte had been in contact to confirm that Emily was not thriving, and she could see very little change. Therefore, as he had already lost his daughter to London and there had been no improvement to her state of mind, he suggested she leave the country for a considerable amount of time to help with her recovery. He proposed a lengthy visit to Vienna. However, Charlotte was unable to accompany Emily due to the endless amount of social engagements in her diary. Lady Leatherby was not in a position to chaperone her daughter as she had not been in good health recently. The one person who was available to travel with Emily was William. Lord Leatherby intended to employ a temporary estate manager while William was out of the country.

William was beside himself with anger. All of these plans had been arranged since he had spoken with his father at breakfast. He refused fiercely; he would not be travelling to Vienna under any circumstances. But his father was very aware of the affection his son held for his younger sister, and he knew that William wouldn't be the one to let her down.

It was less than a week before William was due to leave for Vienna.

***

The following morning, Martha entered the library and was shocked to see William standing alongside the bureau. The family never made an appearance at such an early hour.

"Sorry, sir, I'll come back when you've finished," she said, starting to back out of the room, with Mrs Harvey's stern words echoing in her head.

"No, Martha, stay. I want to speak to you," William said as he rushed to close the door. "Emily isn't recovering very well in London. My father has arranged for an extended holiday—he feels it will be good for her. The only person available to act as chaperone is me. I'm so sorry, it won't be possible for us to have another wonderful day together for a long time."

Martha was surprised how grieved she felt at hearing this news.

"How long will you be away for?" she asked.

"It will be months. How many, I can't be sure. But I will write every week, I promise."

He moved closer, and cupping his hands, he took hold of her face and softly kissed her lips. His touch was warm and gentle, her heart was pounding, and when he stopped, she stood motionless, her eyes still closed.

She could sense his urgency to keep her in his arms. Her heart ached for him to stay. Everything about William's tenderness told her he felt the same.

When she opened her eyes, she smiled lovingly at him and said, "I will look forward to reading your letters, William, and to the day when we can spend time together again."

***

William had reluctantly packed and was ready to leave Leatherby to catch the London train. At Victoria Station, he found Emily surrounded by luggage, anxiously awaiting his arrival with Ethel in tow, who was finding it difficult to control her excitement at the thought of travelling to Europe. Charlotte appeared just in time to wave them off.

From Victoria Station, the journey would take them to the Port of Dover, across the English Channel by steamboat to Calais, then by train from Calais to Paris. The final leg of their journey from Paris to Vienna was aboard the deluxe Orient Express.

After a tiresome journey, William was relieved to be taking his seat for dinner that evening. In less than twenty-four hours, the Orient Express would be steaming its way into Vienna Station. Emily chose not to join him; the journey had taken its toll. She excused herself and decided on an early night, with Ethel attending to her needs. William was quietly relieved and welcomed the peace and quiet.

He entered the dining car to a welcoming array of tables adorned with brilliant white cloths and matching neatly folded napkins, sparkling glasses and gleaming silver cutlery. At the centre of each table was a small, perfectly placed crystal vase, which held a single red rose. He was shown to his seat and provided with a menu. The oysters and fillet of beef with chateau potatoes would most definitely be his choice, followed by chocolate pudding.

The waiter poured a large glass of red wine. William lifted his glass, sat back in his chair and immediately thought of Martha. How he wished she could be with him.

The Orient Express arrived in Vienna late the following afternoon. Their accommodation for the foreseeable future was the Hotel Imperial. It was an impressive building that had originally been built as a private palace for Prince Phillip of Wuerttemberg and his wife. However, the couple did not enjoy their new home for very long. The magnificent building was sold after only five years, at which point it became a hotel.

The lobby dazzled with aristocratic splendour. It was the utmost in grandeur and opulence. There were displays of ornate marble, hand-carved statues, lavish decor and imposing crystal chandeliers. Each one conveyed Viennese elegance. The concierge directed them to the royal staircase, which led to their lavish suites, once the private apartments of the prince and his wife.

William's suite was vast, illuminated by a regal chandelier, which dominated the room. The entire decor triumphed in an overflow of extravagance. William drew back the heavy, plush red velvet drapes and opened the balcony doors. The Vienna skyline was a sight to behold. He took a sharp intake of breath at the impressive architecture displayed before him. Austria was indeed picturesque, and one day, Martha would think so too.

Chapter 16

"Merry Christmas!" Dotty shouted to Martha from the kitchen.

It was Martha's second Christmas at Leatherby Manor, but this year it was very different. Mrs Mead had been informed to prepare for a low-key festive season due to the cold virus spiralling through the household. Charlie, Arthur, Ed and Nell had been confined to their rooms since the day before Christmas Eve. The mere start of a sniffle and Mrs Harvey insisted on lots of fluids and bed rest. Dotty, Elsie and Muriel had already recovered and so had Mr Hampton. Upstairs, Lord and Lady Leatherby were struggling with their recovery. Martha and Mrs Harvey had to date avoided the illness, and according to Mr Hampton, it would take an elephant-sized dose of the virus to incapacitate Mrs Mead; she ploughed on whatever.

Martha could hardly believe that it was Christmas Day and William had left for Vienna six months ago. During that time, she had not received one letter from him. She felt foolish for ever believing he would write to her every week. Martha recalled Mrs Harvey's words: "He just felt sorry for you." How right she had been.

Christmas lunch was very subdued, and the day passed with very little Christmas spirit. Mrs Mead tried her best to put a smile on their faces with her amazing flaming Christmas pudding.

"Well, I thought that would have cheered you all up. You're a right miserable lot, I can tell you," she said, sounding disappointed that her efforts had gone to waste.

By Boxing Day morning, Martha had succumbed to the virus. Her fate was to remain in bed until she felt well enough to return to her duties.

The lead-up to New Year's Eve passed uneventfully. In all the years Mr Hampton had worked at Leatherby, this was the first time the servants' ball had been cancelled. Martha was still unwell, and the rest of the staff were feeling lethargic and lacking in any kind of cheerfulness. New Year's Eve came and went with without any celebrations. They wished each other a happy 1911, and one by one, they said goodnight.

***

Christmas in Vienna had been remarkably different. The temperature had dropped, and William had experienced a cold, snowy festive season. The heart-warming Christmas market was magical. He was drawn to the multicoloured, illuminated stalls with their displays of intricate Christmas decorations and toys. He was fascinated by the hustle and bustle of people indulging in the delights of the festivities. Vienna was known as the "City of Dreams", and he could certainly see why.

He had allowed himself time to tour the numerous museums, attend classical music concerts, and visit the opera and art galleries. The wealth of history Vienna had to offer captivated him, along with the architecture that displayed splendour and prosperity.

It was a new year, and his time in Vienna was coming to an end. Emily had thrived in the six months she had spent away from anything or anybody that reminded her of Henry Enson. It was time to return to England, but William knew in his heart, he would one day return to the City of Dreams.

***

It was the week after New Year, and the only person not to have recovered fully from the virus that had raged through the house was Lady Leatherby. Dr Matthews had paid numerous visits and ordered complete bed rest; he was confident it would aid her recovery. Lady Leatherby had been informed that William and Emily were returning from Vienna, which initially lifted her spirits, until her husband confirmed that Emily intended to remain with Charlotte and Edward in London, much to Charlotte's delight. Emily had written to her father and advised him that if she returned to Leatherby Manor, it would undo her recovery. Lord Leatherby was saddened to hear the news but was relieved that his daughter's state of mind had greatly improved.

***

"Emily, you look positively glowing. Vienna obviously agreed with you," Charlotte said as she rushed to give her niece a hug.

"I feel so much better, Aunt Charlotte. I'm now ready to enjoy all the social events you have planned," Emily replied, smiling at her aunt.

"And William, how did Vienna treat you?" Charlotte asked, turning to look at William, who was relieved to have arrived in England. The return journey had been fraught with delays and constant chatter from Emily and Ethel.

"It's a wonderful city, an experience I shall never forget. You should visit one day, Aunt Charlotte. I guarantee you will fall in love with the wonders of Vienna."

William left Belgrave Square the following morning, eager to return to Leatherby.

"Welcome home, sir," Denton said, as he collected William's luggage and showed him to the car.

"Denton, drive towards the cottage. I want to check on the progress," William instructed. "After six months, there should be a vast improvement."

Denton came to a halt outside the cottage and, furious, William leapt out of the car. The appearance of the cottage had not altered since the day he had left for Vienna. There had been no attempt at re-thatching the roof or the thatch over the porch entrance and the chimney had deteriorated further while he had been away. He pushed open the heavy oak front door to find the inside untouched.

The outbuildings to the rear of the cottage, one of which he intended to occupy as his estate office, had not received any attention. The gardens, both front and back, were overgrown, and the stone wall dividing the back garden from the outhouses had collapsed.

William's anger turned to disappointment and then frustration. He had expected to be in a position to take up occupancy on his return. The cottage was situated a short distance from the lake, and far enough away from the manor for William to take advantage of country living. He'd intended to abandon his father's stifled way of life once and for all and to live as he had done in Scotland with just a cook and a housemaid. He returned to the car feeling deflated.

The usual welcome home party was gathered outside the manor. The higher ranked servants had been summonsed, and his father was patiently awaiting his return. Lord Leatherby frowned as William strode briskly into the house. He briefly acknowledged his father but gave no recognition to the servants.

The staff dispersed, and Mr Hampton followed William and his father into the drawing room.

"Hampton, could you arrange some tea?" Lord Leathery requested while he waited for his son to explain his bad mood.

William looked directly at his father. "I don't want bloody tea; I want an explanation as to why the cottage looks worse than it did before I left for Vienna."

William was finding it difficult to control his temper. He paced up and down the room, waiting for his father's response.

"The only explanation I have is that I put all work on hold until you returned. I thought that—"

"Why? Why would you do that? What were you thinking? Six months on standstill!" William shouted, just as Hampton entered with the tea tray.

Enraged, William stormed out of the drawing room, slamming the door violently behind him.

Just before he left, he heard Hampton, ever unflustered, ask, "Would you like me to pour, my lord?"

William took the stairs two at a time but stopped abruptly when he reached the top. He needed to calm himself before entering his mother's room; she wasn't in good health, and he didn't want to make matters worse. He gently knocked on the door.

"Mother, it's William."

Lady Leatherby's voice sounded faint when she replied. "Come in, William. Please come in."

He was shocked to see his mother looking so frail. There were dark circles underneath her eyes and her complexion was ashen. Usually, she displayed a healthy glow, but not today.

He walked across the room and kissed her cheek, then pulled a chair towards the bed and took his mother's hand. "How are you feeling today?"

"Tired, William, always tired," she said, stroking his face. "Never mind about me. How was Vienna, and how is my lovely daughter?"

"Vienna was magical, and Emily has regained her appetite for life. Henry Enson is no more," William said with confidence.

"And you and your father, William? How are you and your father?"

"Don't concern yourself with us. Just concentrate on getting better."

"But William, I worry about you."

It was obvious his mother was exhausted. William leaned across the bed and kissed her forehead.

"Try to get some rest, Mother," he said, and then he left the room.

Chapter 17

On entering the library, Martha felt she was experiencing déjà vu. William was standing in the exact place he had stood on the morning he had promised to write, all those months ago.

"Hello, Martha," William said. He moved towards her, but the lack of warmth she displayed stopped him in his tracks.

"Good morning, sir," she replied, adding a sharp edge to her tone and trying with all she could muster not to make eye contact.

As he walked towards her, she lifted her head and stared directly at him. "You didn't write. You promised you would write."

William stopped, confused. "I wrote every week, every single week. I wrote about the wonders of Vienna and how much you would love the City of Dreams, I wrote about how magnificent the hotel was, and I wrote how much I was missing you," he said, the words rushing frantically out of him.

"I didn't receive one letter, William, not one. Mrs Harvey was right—the day you drove me to see my family, you just felt sorry for me. I should have listened to her instead of hoping and waiting for your letters. I was just making a fool of myself," she said as the tears escaped. Willing herself to stay composed, she turned and left the room, closing the door behind her.

"But I did write. I did," he said out loud to an empty room.

This was not the homecoming William had envisaged. It was plain to see that Martha wanted nothing more to do with him, and he couldn't blame her—she hadn't received a single letter. He cursed the day he had left for Vienna.

The relationship with his father had not improved, and they spent as little time as possible in each other's company. Lady Leatherby, however, was causing both of them concern. Her appetite had dwindled further, and she had no inclination to leave her bed due to exhaustion. Dr Griffith insisted that bed rest was the answer, but on his last visit, he admitted he felt uneasy as there was very little progress. Due to the paleness of Lady Leatherby's skin, her weakness, extreme fatigue and shortness of breath, he eventually diagnosed anaemia. She was treated with a specialised diet, medication and more bed rest. Gradually, the medication began to take effect, and slowly, Lady Leatherby improved.

"I would like to sit in the drawing room this afternoon. The air is much warmer now spring has arrived, and I do so need a change of scenery," Lady Leatherby announced, as Muriel entered the room.

Muriel was so pleased to hear this request. Steadily and carefully, she assisted Her Ladyship downstairs and made her comfortable in the drawing room.

The room enjoyed extensive views of the immaculate gardens. The sun made its presence known and streamed through the open French doors, encouraging the fragile voile to dance gently in the breeze. Lady Leatherby savoured every moment in the drawing room; its decor had always been her favourite.

"My Lady, it is a welcome sight indeed to see you enjoying the spring sunshine," Hampton said as he placed the tea tray alongside her.

"Thank you, Hampton; I have been cooped upstairs for far too long. I am feeling so much stronger."

There was a marked difference in her appearance. Her pallor looked healthier, and the dark circles under her eyes had all but gone. The fatigue was lessening every day.

"Well, that is good news. Her Ladyship is up and about. Yes, good news indeed," Mrs Mead said when she heard, feeling uplifted.

There had been a gloomy atmosphere downstairs with all the illness, the rift between William and his father, and Her Ladyship having been so unwell. The coronation was looming, and being a staunch royalist, Mrs Mead was convinced the celebrations would put a smile on everybody's face.

Martha found it difficult to show any enthusiasm towards the coronation of George V. She still felt incredibly foolish for allowing herself to think that she had actually meant something to William. It had been a hard lesson to learn, but it was even harder to put him out of her mind, and every day became an effort to ensure their paths didn't cross. It was a blessing that William spent most of his time at the cottage, and he barely graced the manor house with his presence.

June 22nd was coronation day. Lord and Lady Leatherby intended to visit Emily in London and witness the coronation at the same time. Lady Leatherby was feeling much stronger and was anxious to visit her daughter.

Mrs Mead was driving everybody downstairs to distraction with her continual chatter about the coronation celebrations. She purchased Union Jack bunting as well as bunting with an image of King George V, flags printed with "God save the King" and two larger flags with an image of King George V and Queen Mary. Charlie had been given strict instructions of exactly where to place the decorations.

"This is worse than lighting all those blessed candles on that monster of a Christmas tree," Charlie said as he repositioned the flags for the third time at Mrs Mead's instructions.

Lord and Lady Leatherby had bought every member of staff a coronation commemorative mug. It was a thoughtful gesture but completely wasted on some of the servants, especially Charlie and the other lads. Mrs Mead, however, was thrilled. She had no intention of ever using it. She gave it a place of honour, carefully positioning it in the centre of the mantelpiece, much to everybody's horror. The cream china mug, edged in blue with a picture of the King and Queen on either side of a large gaudy royal crest, looked completely out of place, but nobody dared say a word or move it, not even Mrs Harvey or Mr Hampton.

When all the household duties had been completed, Mrs Mead ensured the celebrations got off the ground. It was a glorious day, and she was adamant that the large table from the servants' hall should be moved into the courtyard along with the reams of bunting and flags. All of Charlie's hard work putting the decorations up inside now had to be moved outdoors. The table was laid with a buffet fit for royalty, the sun shone, and the bunting and flags waved in the breeze. Mrs Mead insisted they toast the new king and queen. Proudly turning to face the largest flag, which portrayed an image of the king, she raised her glass and proclaimed, "God save the King."

Chapter 18

There was still much work to be done at the cottage. The garden, however, was beginning to take shape thanks to Albie. William spent many a long hour working side by side with him, sometimes late into the evening.

The makeshift office deeply frustrated William. It was untidy and disorganised and virtually impossible to locate the paperwork required to run the estate smoothly.

"Everything all right, sir?" Mr Hampton asked as an angry William marched past him and into the library, completely ignoring Hampton's concern.

He was focused on searching for the much-needed paperwork. There was a possibility it could be in his father's bureau. The fact that the bureau was locked infuriated William even more—it was never locked, and he had no idea where the key was kept. In his irate state, he forced the bureau open with a paper knife. As the lock released and the bureau sprung open, a deluge of letters fell to the floor. William was aghast. Every single envelope was addressed to Martha. His letters sent from Vienna had been intercepted. All the mail that arrived at the manor was delivered to the servants' area and handed to Mr Hampton. The distribution of the mail upstairs and downstairs was his responsibility. It was clear to William that Hampton had notified Lord Leatherby the minute the very first letter from Vienna had arrived.

He gathered every single letter and placed them on top of the bureau then rang for Hampton. The minute

Mr Hampton entered the library, his eyes darted to the pile of letters.

Although William was seething, he tried his utmost to remain calm. "I would like you to explain why the letters I sent Martha from Vienna are unopened and locked away in my father's bureau."

"Your father requested that I collect every letter received," Hampton explained, quite calmly.

"My father would not have had any knowledge of the correspondence between myself and Martha had you not informed him—am I correct, Hampton?"

"Yes, sir. That is correct."

Hampton's reaction was bordering the lines of insubordination.

William couldn't bear to look at him any longer. He was astounded that this man standing in front of him, poised and unconcerned, had felt the need to perform such a spiteful and despicable deed. It was no secret that Hampton's loyalty to Lord Leatherby had no boundaries, and he endeavoured to serve His Lordship with the utmost commitment.

"That's all, Hampton. Ask Martha to make her way to the library as soon as possible," William said, full of intent for her to witness the huge amount of correspondence she had never had the privilege to receive.

"Martha isn't here, sir. Her brother arrived last night to escort her home, as her young sister is gravely ill. They left immediately."

This was devastating news. Instantly, William was distraught—he needed to be at Martha's side.

His words became frantic. "Tell Denton to bring the car to the front of the house, now," he demanded.

He made the dash to Martha's home. When he arrived, the front door of the little cottage was ajar. He knocked but didn't receive a reply. Slowly, he pushed the door open and entered the cottage to find the door to the front room open wide. He stood in the doorway with a heavy heart and fearing the worse. Martha was sobbing, and her brother was trying his utmost to comfort her. It could not have been more dissimilar from the last time he stood in the cosy little front room.

"Martha," he called softly.

Martha pulled away from her brother's hold, and as if in a daze, she walked towards William. He wrapped his arms tightly around her; she nestled into him and cried bitterly. No words from him would console her. He could only cradle her, letting her cry and then soothe her tears.

Tilly had lost her battle with scarlet fever, a disease that afflicted children between the ages of five and fifteen. She was just ten years old. Martha's parents were heartbroken and in shock but relieved that Martha had arrived in time. Despite the sorrowful mood hanging heavy over them, they remained just as hospitable as William's previous visit, and he was invited to eat with them before his journey back to Leatherby.

"Nice of you to come, lad," Martha's father said. "And you will be very welcome at the funeral."

"Thank you, Mr Thomson," William replied, wondering at how composed the man was when his heart was surely breaking.

Martha had made the decision to remain at home until after Tilly's funeral. William wanted so much to tell her about the letters from Vienna, but it wasn't the right time. He held her close before he left and assured her he would return for the funeral. She stood on the doorstep and watched him drive away until the car was out of sight.

He drove back to Leatherby with his mind full of thoughts of Martha and the sadness that was now engulfing the little cottage.

"Good evening, sir. Lord and Lady Leatherby have returned from London and are in the dining room. Will you be joining them?" Mr Hampton enquired as William entered the hall.

"No, Hampton, I won't be joining them," he replied and headed directly for the library, where he collected the letters. He then made his way across the hall and burst into the dining room.

"Good gracious, William. What on earth is the rush?" Lady Leatherby said, looking at her son in amazement.

"I presume Hampton has informed you of this morning's events. So, you won't be surprised to see these." William scowled as he launched the letters across the dining room table towards his father.

Lady Leatherby gasped, raising a hand to her breast. She looked at the letters with confusion.

"I don't understand, William. These letters are addressed to Martha Thomson," Lady Leatherby said as she studied a handful of the envelopes.

"That's right, Mother. Father intercepted them; therefore, she never received any. Not one."

"This nonsense has to stop," Lord Leatherby bellowed, thumping his fist on the table as he stood up. "The girl is a housemaid; she is employed downstairs, William—do you understand?"

William turned to Charlie, Arthur and Mr Hampton, who were still in attendance in the dining room. "You are all dismissed."

"But sir—" began Hampton.

"I said you are dismissed." This time, William almost growled the instruction, and all three servants left the room.

"George, the most important thing to me is the happiness of my children," Lady Leatherby said, looking directly at her husband. "If Martha makes William happy, so be it. Life is too short."

Lord Leatherby looked at his wife then turned to William. "Yes, I suppose it is... I have watched Emily suffer. She was so very unhappy. It truly broke my heart." He walked towards his son and extended his arm to shake his hand.

"Your mother is right. You have my blessing."

This approval had been a long time coming. Tears welled in William's eyes. He turned to his mother; her face was alight with happiness. Within an instant, his life felt complete. There had been so much heartache at Leatherby Manor, and now, the sun was shining on his future. A future spent with Martha.

"Thank you," William replied, shaking his father's hand with vigour.

"We shall retire to the drawing room," Lady Leatherby said. "William, please ask Martha to join us. I would very much like to speak with her."

"That's not possible, Mother, I'm afraid. She is at home with her family. Sadly, her younger sister has passed away due to scarlet fever. She intends to return after the funeral."

"See, George. Life is too short," Lady Leatherby replied, and she left the dining room.

Chapter 19

The outburst in the dining room soon became common knowledge downstairs courtesy of Charlie. Nell was happy to hear that Martha had received letters from William. It had worried her to see her friend so unhappy. Mrs Mead wanted to know every little detail of Master William's outburst and repeatedly asked Charlie questions. Mrs Harvey felt a sense of guilt, as she had been aware of the conspiracy between Mr Hampton and Lord Leatherby. Arthur and Ed didn't seem interested—good luck to Martha, they both thought. Dotty loved the romance of it all and was already hoping that one day she too would meet her prince, until Mrs Mead had to remind her that Master William was not a prince and the possibility of her ever meeting a prince was none. Elsie appeared oblivious to it all, and Muriel put pen to paper as soon as she could to keep Ethel informed and up to date.

William attended Tilly's funeral as promised, and after a difficult family farewell, Martha returned to Leatherby. William was intent on showing her the cottage. The thatch roof was complete, and the window frames had been painted pale blue. Albie had planted a rose bush that, in time, would display wonderful pink roses which would surround the newly repaired thatched porch. Martha was struck by the beauty of it all. The inside didn't match the pristine appearance of the garden; there was still some work to be completed, but she could see the potential, and she adored it.

"I have something to show you," William said as he opened a drawer to reveal the letters sent from Vienna.

Martha stepped forward to take a closer look. Confused, she looked to William for an explanation.

He described in detail the reason she had not received the letters. Hurt rose in her, and her face fell. To think that Mr Hampton could have done something so awful made her sad. But in her heart, she was relieved to know William had written.

He bundled the letters together and handed them to her.

"I want you to read every single one," he said. "I want you to know exactly how I feel."

***

Martha returned to the manor house and to her duties as a housemaid. So he could spend time with her, William had made his presence known downstairs. It had been unsettling for everybody with the master popping in and out, but they soon became comfortable with his comings and goings. Everyone that is, except Mr Hampton and Mrs Harvey.

"I find it hard to believe that His Lordship is at all happy with any of this arrangement," Mr Hampton commented to Mrs Harvey.

"It's not for us to interfere. We have always thought the master was not cut from the same cloth as His Lordship, and we know for sure now," was Mrs Harvey's curt reply.

They both struggled to accept William making himself at home in the servants' hall and enjoying the company of Charlie, Arthur and Ed. William regularly joined the staff for meals, and he seemed to relish the happy, relaxed atmosphere. It all became a little too much for Mr Hampton when William arrived downstairs one afternoon to inform Martha that his mother would like to speak with her in the drawing room.

***

"There's no need to be nervous," William said brightly as he led Martha up the stairs. "My mother really is very nice."

Martha followed him hesitantly into the drawing room. The entire situation felt surreal, and she was nervous; she couldn't help it.

"Good afternoon, Martha. Come here and make yourself comfortable, my dear," Lady Leatherby said as she patted the space next to her on the sofa.

Martha apprehensively walked across the room and took the offered seat.

"My son tells me that you make him happy, and I can certainly see why," Lady Leatherby said, taking in every detail of Martha's appearance and smiling softly. "I want you to know that you have my blessing. If my son is happy, then so am I. And you mustn't worry about Lord Leatherby—he will eventually be less miserable about the situation. He just doesn't know it yet."

Martha and William both smiled, which is more than could be said for Hampton as he placed the tea tray alongside them.

Below stairs, the excitement was building as the Christmas preparations were starting to get into full swing. This year, however, saw William very much become part of the furniture downstairs. He and Martha grew closer, and their happiness was evident for everybody to see, including Mr Hampton and Mrs Harvey.

Martha's love of Christmas and the thought of spending time with William filled her with excitement and delight. They spent precious time in the cottage decorating the Christmas tree, which had been placed alongside the inglenook fireplace. The flames from the fire soared and sent a golden glow throughout the cosy front room. One by one, Martha and William placed fragile glass baubles on the branches and lit the carefully placed candles.

Gently, William lifted Martha high enough to reach the top of the Christmas tree. Taking great care, she placed the ornate silver fairy in her rightful position. As William lowered her, he kept his arms tightly around her waist, and pulling her towards him, he kissed her softly. Then, surrounded by the flickering radiance of the candles, he said, "Martha Thomson, will you marry me?"

Chapter 20

It was to be a spring wedding. Lady Leatherby was ecstatic to hear the news. Her husband, however, not quite as much.

The bride- and groom-to-be had made the decision to hold the wedding breakfast in the servants' hall. They were determined it would be as low-key as possible. There was to be none of the pomp and ceremony usually associated with an aristocratic wedding. The only guests invited were the staff, Lord and Lady Leatherby, Martha's parents and her brother, Tommy. Charlotte, Edward and Emily would also receive an invite, but William doubted very much they would attend when they were informed of the wedding breakfast venue.

As soon as Martha had said yes, the journey was made to visit her parents. It was a bitterly cold January day, so they were relieved to arrive at the cottage and to be greeted by the cosiness of the fire in the little front room.

"Come in and warm up," Martha's mother said as she ushered them both into the cottage. "Your dad and Tommy aren't home from the pit yet, love."

"How are you, Mam?" Martha asked as she gave her mother a big hug.

"Oh, you know, love, you know," her mother said, sounding as if in her heart she knew she would never be able to come to terms with the loss of her little girl.

As soon as Martha's dad and her brother arrived home, William approached Mr Thomson to ask him if he could marry his daughter.

"Indeed you can, lad, indeed you can," he said with the proudest smile on his face.

Martha's mother put both hands to her face in shock and became very tearful.

Martha's father and brother were black from head to toe with coal dust, but it didn't stop everybody hugging each other and celebrating the good news.

Martha turned to her mother and said affectionately, "I would really like to be married in the dress you wore on your wedding day, Mam. You do still have it, don't you?"

Martha's mother was so overwhelmed she couldn't speak. She just looked at her daughter and nodded. Out of sight of William, Martha was handed a box that had stored the precious dress for many years. With great care, Martha lifted the treasured wedding dress out of the box. It was just as lovely as in the wedding photo on the wall in the front room.

"It's perfect, Mam, just perfect," she said, knowing how proud she would feel when she walked down the aisle to stand alongside William.

***

There were just four months before the wedding day. Mrs Mead had started preparations for the wedding cake. It wasn't going to be on the scale of the one she had baked for Emily; this cake would be elegant but modest. The wedding breakfast was to be a cold buffet and the flowers a collection of garden and wild spring blooms.

Lady Leatherby questioned William regarding the honeymoon. He had no intention of revealing his plans to his mother for fear that she would inadvertently reveal the destination to Martha and the surprise would be ruined.

Lady Leatherby suggested that as Emily no longer required her wardrobe of clothing that had been abandoned when she left for London, Martha was welcome to any items that she saw fit. After all, she was going to require a complete collection for her honeymoon. Martha was grateful for her soon-to-be mother-in-law's thoughtfulness and generosity. She asked Nell to accompany her to Emily's room to help decide on appropriate outfits.

Emily had left behind the most fashionable of outfits, all of which had hardly been worn. Martha and Emily were both very petite, and Nell watched in awe as Martha tried on a selection of chic, overly expensive designs.

"You look beautiful, Martha. I'm so happy for you," she said, as she helped fasten the delicate pearl and satin buttons.

The evening gown Martha was wearing was navy velvet with a gold satin sash and gold teardrop beads edging the neckline and the hem. Navy shoes encrusted in gold sequins and a pair of elbow-length evening gloves in navy velvet completed the outfit. She looked the epitome of elegance.

The evening before the wedding arrived, the last night Martha would spend in the attic bedroom. The tiny room had been her home for almost three years, but on her return from their honeymoon, she would begin her new life in the adorable little thatched cottage.

So much had happened since the day she took up the position of housemaid. She had lots of happy memories, but she would never forget the sadness of losing her friend. She glanced at the little glass vase Rosie had bought her for Christmas and sighed, wishing Rosie could share her wedding day with her.

Mrs Mead had put the finishing touches to the wedding cake. It was just two tiers high and decorated with a blue ribbon placed around both cakes. An array of tiny white flowers had been iced with the utmost precision and intricately set to resemble small posies.

"Mrs Mead, thank you—it's wonderful," Martha said, as she stretched out her arms to give her a big thank-you hug.

"I'm glad you like it, lass. We just need to add the flowers to the top and it will be all done and dusted," Mrs Mead said.

Bluebells were laid across the top of the cake, and the effect was striking.

Carefully, the cake was positioned in the centre of the large table in the servant's hall. Then, much to Martha's surprise, Mrs Mead removed the gaudy coronation mug from the mantelpiece and asked Martha to collect the little glass vase in her room. When she returned, Mrs Mead arranged the remaining bluebells in the vase and placed it on the mantelpiece. It was a lovely touch which Martha truly appreciated.

"Mrs Mead, that is a beautiful cake indeed," Mrs Harvey said as she entered the servants' hall. "Martha, could I have a word with you in my room?"

A knot of apprehension in her stomach, Martha followed Mrs Harvey to her parlour.

"Martha, I know we haven't been on the best of footing for a little while, but I want to let you know I can see that you and the master are very happy," Mrs Harvey said. "I was wrong to judge, and I am sorry. So, I would like to wish you lots of continued happiness, and please accept this as a gift from me to you." She handed Martha a small, red, square box, around which was tied a thin white satin ribbon.

Martha untied the ribbon and opened the box. She gasped.

"I can't accept this, Mrs Harvey," she said, staring at the gold locket placed on a red velvet mount.

"I was my mother's, and as I don't have a daughter to pass it on to, I would very much like you to have it."

"I shall wear it tomorrow on my wedding day. Thank you," Martha said, and she leaned across to kiss Mrs Harvey on the cheek.

Chapter 21

When Martha woke, her eyes were instantly drawn to the wedding dress hanging from the old and tired-looking wardrobe. This time tomorrow, she would no longer be Martha Thomson.

"Martha Leatherby," she said out loud. She liked the sound of it very much.

"Martha, can I come in?" Nell called. She had arrived to help the bride prepare for her big day. Elsie and Dotty had arranged a breakfast tray for Martha, and as an extra special touch, they had placed a small bunch of yellow primroses on the tray for luck.

Downstairs, everything was in hand. Mrs Mead, Elsie and Dotty wouldn't be attending the wedding service; they were remaining at the manor to ensure the buffet was laid in preparation for the guests' return. Martha's family had received an invite from Lord and Lady Leatherby to stay at the manor house the night before the wedding. However, they graciously declined, as they felt more comfortable renting a room in the village pub.

In the drawing room, William paced back and forth. He was nervous, and it had taken him by surprise. He had planned the day and the honeymoon to perfection, but he hadn't accounted for nerves. He would be relieved when they were man and wife and setting off on their new life together.

Lord Leatherby entered the room and poured them both a drink. Handing William the glass, he said, "I know

I haven't made things easy for you, son, and I should never have interfered with the letters from Vienna, but I would dearly like to think you have forgiven me. I love your mother more today than I did all those years ago, and I can't imagine what my life would have been like without her. So, I wish for you and Martha everything your mother and I have had: never-ending love and happiness."

The two men clinked glasses, then William announced, "Drink up. We have a wedding to go to."

***

"Martha, you look just perfect," Nell said wistfully as she fastened the gold locket before making her way to join the rest of the staff, who were about to begin their walk to the church.

Martha glanced at her reflection in the mirror. The ivory silk-satin dress was exquisite. The fitted bodice was nipped in at the waist and covered in delicate lace and tiny clusters of miniature pearls. Silk ribbon was pleated around the scooped neckline, adding a soft, feminine touch. It complemented the gold locket beautifully. Three-quarter puff sleeves were gathered at the elbow and tied with petite silk bows, matching the bows that edged the hem of the sweeping skirt and the rounded train. Nell had teased Martha's hair into a loose braid. The finishing touch was the meticulously placed, star-shaped flowers throughout the braid. The white wood anemones were a striking contrast to Martha's vibrant auburn locks. She stepped into a pair of ivory satin shoes with a small block heel, each of which was decorated with a pearl-covered bow. Then, taking one last look at her little attic bedroom, she closed the door for the last time.

She cautiously made her way down the staircase. Waiting at the foot of the stairs with his back to her was her father. He hadn't heard her approaching.

"Dad," she whispered.

He turned quickly to face her.

"Lass, you look a picture. You really do," he said as he walked towards her, offering her his hand.

"Martha, you looks like a real princess—don't she, Elsie?" Dotty said, staring at Martha in utter amazement.

"Look at me, crying like a baby, I am," Mrs Mead said. "And Dotty's right, you do look like a princess."

Dotty handed Martha her bridal flowers: a posy of bluebells, tulips and miniature daffodils tied with a blue silk ribbon.

"Here you are, lass," Mrs Mead said, passing Martha a pure white handkerchief edged in lace. She had embroidered it with what was to be Martha's new initials: M L.

"Thank you, Mrs Mead. That is so thoughtful," Martha said as she carefully tucked the handkerchief into the centre of her bridal flowers.

***

Lord and Lady Leatherby and William had arrived at the quaint village church. The staff were milling around outside, waiting for the upstairs guests to take their seats before the downstairs guests could enter the church. Tommy, Martha's brother, was enjoying Charlie's banter. Charlie being Charlie was keeping everybody amused. Martha's mother was happily chatting with Mrs Harvey and Albie. It was a surprisingly warm April morning with just a slight breeze, the ideal weather for a wedding.

As William walked towards the church entrance, he heard a familiar voice call his name. When he turned around, Emily was running towards him. Behind her, Ethel was making a beeline for the other servants, no doubt to catch up with all the gossip.

"You came," William said, full of emotion at seeing his sister.

"How could I miss my favourite brother's wedding?" Emily replied, while crushing him with a hug.

Following behind Emily were Charlotte and Edward. William was amazed; he'd been certain they wouldn't be attending.

"William, I need to speak with Hampton about the catering arrangements," Charlotte announced, while frantically scanning the guests, trying to locate him.

"The catering arrangements are as follows: we all eat downstairs, Aunt Charlotte."

"Well, really, William. Your grandmother will be turning in her grave. Now, where am I seated, I hope—"

"Do be quiet, woman," Edward said as he steered his wife towards the church entrance.

***

Denton arrived back at the manor house in readiness to chauffeur the bride. Martha took her father's arm, and he gently guided his precious daughter towards the waiting car. With tears in his eyes, he knew she was about to embark on a journey that would take her to the next chapter of her life. And from the bottom of his heart, he wished his darling girl all the love and happiness in the world.

The car came to a halt outside the church. All the guests had now taken their seats, eager to witness the ceremony.

Martha stepped out of the car into the April sunshine and took hold of her father's arm. When they reached the church entrance, she composed herself and took a deep breath. At that point, the powerful chords of the organ burst into play, radiating through the little church, signalling her arrival. Martha adoringly looked for William; she saw him instantly, patiently waiting for her.

Martha's father turned to her. "Ready, lass?"

She nodded, and they began the emotional walk for her to take her place alongside William. All eyes were on Martha as she glided down the aisle. William turned around. He was hypnotised; his bride looked radiant, and she was glowing with happiness.

Martha's mother, along with the majority of the guests, was seen to have a tear in her eye. Her heart was bursting with love for her beautiful daughter, and she felt so very proud. But it was tinged with sadness that Tilly wasn't there to see her big sister on her special day.

After the service, the church bells sounded, the sun shone, and the love William and Martha had for each other was evident for all to see.

Back at the manor, Mrs Mead was waiting anxiously for the arrival of the wedding party. The buffet had been laid to perfection; even Charlotte relented and relished in the feast. Mr Hampton and the two footmen kept everybody's glasses topped up, and Dotty and Elsie provided a constant relay of food. Before the happy couple left for their honeymoon, there were lots of cheers and good wishes as they cut the cake.

William was reminded by Denton that they had a train to catch. Charlie and Arthur collected their luggage just as soon as William and Martha had discarded their wedding attire. Martha emerged wearing a long navy and white striped cotton dress and straw hat edged in navy ribbon. It was the perfect going-away outfit.

There was much hugging and well-wishing from everybody, including Mr Hampton, who couldn't quite bring himself to apologise for his involvement with the letters. But he did shake William's hand and wished them both a happy honeymoon.

On their way to the station, Martha asked, "Denton, please could you stop here?"

Picking up her bridal flowers, she quickly ran the short distance into the graveyard. Tenderly, she placed the flowers on Rosie's grave. Then, blowing her a kiss, she ran back to the car.

At the end of the train journey, the immense amount of luggage was loaded into a taxi for the journey to the hotel. William quietly spoke to the driver out of earshot of Martha, asking him to take a short detour.

As the taxi began to draw closer to the destination, William said, "Close your eyes, Martha, and don't open them until I tell you."

The taxi stopped, and William guided Martha out of the car.

"You can open them now," he said softly.

She opened her eyes and was greeted in all its glory by the magnificent RMS Titanic.

Slipping his arm around her waist and drawing her closer, William whispered, "Tomorrow we sail for New York."

Epilogue

RMS Titanic departed Southampton to begin her maiden voyage to New York on 10th April 1912, just after midday. Passengers boarded at Cherbourg in France and then Queenstown in Ireland, after which Titanic proceeded with her journey that should have seen her dock in New York early on April 17th.

The Titanic was the largest and most luxurious liner of her time. Passengers and crew believed that due to her immense size and the technological advancements present on the magnificent liner, she was unsinkable.

A total of 1,300 passengers left Southampton on that fateful journey, along with 900 crew members. Tragically, Titanic was never destined to complete her maiden voyage. Despite sailing on calm seas and under a clear moonless sky, and regardless of having received iceberg warnings, she steamed full speed into a field of icebergs, striking one at 11:50 p.m. on April 14th. The impressive, 882 foot long, elaborate and imposing ship received from the iceberg's jagged underwater spur a 300-foot gash that slashed the hull below the ship's waterline.

In the sheer chaos and panic that followed, the lifeboats were not filled to capacity. Each was capable of carrying sixty-eight passengers; sadly, only a small proportion of boats launched were full. The ship had set sail with only twenty lifeboats. Calculations show that even if every lifeboat had been fully occupied, there was still only enough space for half the amount of souls on board Titanic.

In compliance with the law at sea, women and children were loaded into the lifeboats first. Men heartbreakingly said goodbye to their wives and children. Families became separated; however, some gave up their position in the lifeboat to remain with their loved ones. The light flickered for the last time on the Titanic, and at 2:20 a.m. on April 15th, just two hours and forty minutes after the fateful collision, the mighty liner sank to the depths of the ocean.

The RMS Carpathia responded to the SOS distress call. Sadly, it took three and a half hours to arrive at Titanic's location, by which time she had already sunk. Carpathia embarked on a four-hour rescue operation. By 8:15 a.m., just 705 survivors were rescued. 1,500 perished in the freezing waters of the Atlantic Ocean.

There were 175 first-class male passengers, of which 57 survived.

First-class female passengers amounted to 144, of which 140 survived.

There were six children in first class. Five survived.

Amongst the second-class passengers, all twenty-four children survived.

At Southampton, seventy-nine third-class children boarded Titanic, fifty-two of which lost their young lives.

Sadly, only fourteen second-class male passengers survived. 154 perished.

Ninety-three second-class female passengers set sail on the ill-fated ship, of which eighty survived.

The greatest loss to life was in third class. Just seventy-five men survived the disaster from a total of 462.

There were 165 third-class female passengers on board. Just seventy-six were saved.

The enquiry into the sinking of Titanic was held in London from 2nd May to 3rd July 1912.

On 30th July 1912, the final report was published. The report confirmed the sole reason for the sinking of Titanic was the collision with the iceberg. This had occurred due to the ship travelling at a dangerously fast speed in icy waters. It was not due to any inherent flaws in the ship.

The sinking of this magnificent ship RMS Titanic was one of the worst maritime disasters during peacetime.

Author Profile

Judith Ellis's hometown is Swansea, South Wales, where she has always lived and worked until deciding to retire in September 2020.

Retirement has given her the time to pursue her love of writing. In May 2021, her first children's book, Millie Finds a Feather, was published, and in 2022, she has poured all her energy into writing Leatherby Manor.

Photography is also a passion of hers, and as Swansea has the most wonderful coastline (although sadly not such wonderful weather), she enjoys many an hour clicking away at the breathtaking views, come rain or shine.

She lives with her partner of over twenty years. They have two daughters, both of whom have fled the nest for quite some time and are busy building careers of their own.

Her aim when writing Leatherby Manor was to transport the reader back to the early twentieth century and immerse them in this glorious era. She has truly enjoyed writing Leatherby, and would like to think her goal has been achieved.

***

What Did You Think of Leatherby Manor?

A big thank you for purchasing this book. It means a lot that you chose this book specifically from such a wide range on offer. I do hope you enjoyed it.

Book reviews are incredibly important for an author. All feedback helps them improve their writing for future projects and for developing this edition. If you are able to spare a few minutes to post a review on Amazon, that would be much appreciated.

Publisher Information

Rowanvale Books provides publishing services to independent authors, writers and poets all over the globe. We deliver a personal, honest and efficient service that allows authors to see their work published, while remaining in control of the process and retaining their creativity. By making publishing services available to authors in a cost-effective and ethical way, we at Rowanvale Books hope to ensure that the local, national and international community benefits from a steady stream of good quality literature.

For more information about us, our authors or our publications, please get in touch.

www.rowanvalebooks.com
info@rowanvalebooks.com